48 Hours To Die

(An Anthony Stone Novel)

SILK WHITE

Good2Go Publishing

ISBN: 978-0990869436

Copyright ©2015 by Silk White

Published 2015 by Good2Go Publishing

7311 W. Glass Lane • Laveen, AZ 85339

www.good2gopublishing.com

twitter @good2gobooks

G2G@good2gopublishing.com

Facebook.com/good2gopublishing

ThirdLane Marketing: Brian James

Brian@good2gopublishing.com

Cover design: Davida Baldwin

Books by This Author

10 Secrets To Publishing Success

Married To Da Streets

Never Be The Same

Stranded

Sweet Pea's Tough Choices (Children's Book)

Tears of a Hustler

Tears of a Hustler 2

Tears of a Hustler 3

Tears of a Hustler 4

Tears of a Hustler 5

Tears of a Hustler 6

Teflon Queen

Teflon Queen 2

Teflon Queen 3

Teflon Queen 4

Time Is Money (An Anthony Stone Novel)

48 Hours to Die (An Anthony Stone Novel)

<u>Acknowledgments</u>

To all of you who are reading this, thank you for stepping inside the bookstore, stopping by the library, or downloading a copy of 48 Hours To Die. I hope you have enjoyed this read from top to bottom. My goal is to get better and better with each story. I want to thank everyone for all their love and support. It is definitely appreciated! Now without further ado Ladies and Gentleman, I give you *48 Hours To Die*. Enjoy!

$iLK WHiTE

48 HOURS TO DIE
(An Anthony Stone Novel)

48 HƷURS TO DIE

PROLOGUE

Mary sat in the living room on her couch enjoying a glass of wine. She had been laying around the house all day since Tuesdays were her only day off. On nights like this, Mary wished that she had a boyfriend, but right now, she was focused on her career instead, so a boyfriend would have to wait. Mary laid across the couch when she heard what sounded like someone tapping on the window near the kitchen. Mary quickly sat up and muted the TV to make sure the wine wasn't playing tricks on her. She listened carefully for a few seconds, once she was sure that no one was tapping on the window she turned the TV back up. Mary sipped on her wine when she heard the tapping sound again. She slowly stood to her feet, walked over towards the kitchen window, and peeked outside.

BANG!

BANG!

BANG!

The loud banging on the front door startled Mary, causing her to drop her glass of wine on the kitchen floor. She slowly inched her way towards the front door when the loud banging continued.

BANG!

BANG!

BANG!

"Who is it?" Mary called out nervously.

"The police!" A strong voice on the other side of the door boomed. Mary slowly unlocked the door, but made sure she left the chain lock on as she opened the door just a crack so she could see out.

On the other side of the door stood a handsome dark skinned man in a police uniform. "Can I help you?" Mary asked as she noticed it was pouring down raining behind the police officer.

"Good evening ma'am." The officer tipped his hat. "I got a

call about a serial killer that goes by the name Uncle Sam," he paused. "He's been spotted somewhere in this area, so make sure you lock your door and all your windows ma'am," he turned to leave when Mary stopped him.

"Wait!" She said as she removed the chain lock from the door. "I heard a few noises outside of my house would you mind checking around my house for me? If it's not too much trouble,"

The officer smiled, "No trouble at all ma'am, I'll be back in a second,"

Mary closed the door and breathed a sigh of relief. That was the only bad thing about her living alone, if anything bad was to happen there was no one there to protect her. She walked back over towards the kitchen and began cleaning up the broken wine glass when she heard another knock at the door. Mary walked and opened the door happy to see the police officer standing on the other side of the door. "Is everything alright?"

"I didn't see anyone around the back of the house," the officer said. "But I did find this leaning up against the side of the house," he showed her a shiny ax. "I guess I must have scared the guy off or something,"

Mary had a frightened look on her face. "Bu... but what if he comes back?"

"Do you have a relative or friend you can stay with for a couple of days?" The officer asked. "Only for a few days, just until the suspect is captured,"

"Yes I have a cousin that doesn't live too far away from here,"

"Great," the officer turned to leave when, Mary stopped him.

"Do you mind waiting here while I go and pack a few things?" Mary asked. "I promise it'll only take a second."

The officer smiled. "Sure no problem,"

"Make yourself at home," Mary said before disappearing upstairs. She grabbed a small duffle bag and packed as many things inside of it as she could. Mary then ran to her closet and threw on a pair of jeans, a shirt, and slipped her feet in a pair of flip-flops, then made her way back downstairs.

When Mary stepped foot back downstairs she noticed that the officer was nowhere in sight. "Hello? Anybody there?" She called out looking around the house. "Where did he go that fast?" Mary wondered, hoping that nothing bad had happened while she was upstairs. Out of nowhere, Mary felt a tap on her shoulder that caused her to almost jump out of her skin. "Oh my god!" She yelled holding her chest. "You scared the crap out of me!" She said looking at the officer.

"Sorry," The officer apologized. "I didn't mean to scare you,"

"You can't just be disappearing like that,"

"Sorry I had to use the bathroom," the officer apologized again.

Mary calmed herself down, and grabbed her bag. "Can we go now?" She headed for the door. Mary grabbed the doorknob and stopped dead in her tracks when she heard a growling sound coming from behind her.

The officer waited until Mary reached the door before he grabbed the ax with two hands and swung it like a baseball bat.

"Arggggh!" Mary howled as she collapsed and saw her leg sitting on the floor next to her detached from her body. She looked up at the officer with fear in her eyes. "W...wh... why are doing this?"

"I'm sorry, I forgot to introduce myself," The officer smiled, and extended his hand. "My friends call me Reggie, but you can call me Uncle Sam."

48 HOURS TO DIE
(An Anthony Stone Novel)

48 HƷURS TO DIE

CHAPTER 1

K nock! Knock! Knock!
An elderly woman answered the door, and she stuck her head out. "May I help you?" She asked in soft voice.

"How you doing ma'am? I'm detective Anthony Stone; I received a call about a disturbance?"

"Oh yes I heard loud screams coming from next door," the old lady explained. "Which is strange because my neighbor lives over there alone and rarely has company over there."

"When you say screams did you mean like in passion or did you mean..."

"Oh no it wasn't those type of screams," she shook her head. "It was the type of screams that would make me call the police."

"I see," Anthony Stone said as he looked over at the house next door. "Ma'am I need you to go back inside and lock your door while I go over there and check it out."

"Be careful," the old lady said then, disappeared back inside of her house.

Anthony Stone headed over towards the house next door with caution. He reached the front of the house and saw that the front door was left slightly ajar. Stone whipped his 9mm out of his holster in a snapping motion; he then called in for back up as he entered the house through the front door. The inside of the house was dark and looked real creepy. Anthony Stone pulled out his Maglite and held it just above his gun. The light from the flash light guided him through the house. He stopped when he almost slipped on something wet on the floor. Anthony Stone looked down and saw that he was standing in a puddle of blood. "Shit!" He cursed. Over on the wall he spotted a light switch. He hit the lights and immediately he couldn't believe his eyes. All scattered throughout the living room were a woman's body parts.

Anthony Stone covered his nose as he continued to search the house making sure that no one else was inside. When he was done checking the house, he returned back to the living room. There was blood everywhere, Anthony Stone looked down and saw what looked to be chopped off fingers, and toes scattered all throughout the floor. Over on the coffee table he spotted an envelope that had the number three written on it. Anthony Stone grabbed the envelope and opened it.

"If you're reading this, then that means once again the police weren't able to save or protect the innocent. The police job is to protect and serve but all they seem to do is serve and protect themselves. I will continue to keep on killing and force you pigs to do your job.

Sincerely yours: Uncle Sam."

Anthony Stone finished reading the letter just as his backup arrived. He knew the media was going to have a field day with this story. This was the third killing in the last two months.

"Stone!" Captain Fisher called out.

"Hey captain I found this on the coffee table," Stone handing his captain the letter. Caption Fisher read the letter then shook his head. He was trying his best to get a wrap on the murders before the media began scaring the public with talks of a serial killer.

"I need you to find this asshole!" Captain Fisher barked. "This asshole is playing us like a violin,"

Each murder was worse than the last one and he knew if Anthony Stone didn't catch this scumbag, he would surely strike again.

"Don't worry about it captain, I'm on it," Anthony Stone said looking down at the letter again. Whoever this Uncle Sam guy was, it was clear that he had a serious problem with police and wanted to make every law enforcement agent out there look like a fool.

Anthony Stone exited the house and was immediately swarmed by the media.

"Is it safe to say that we have a serial killer on the loose?" A reporter asked shoving a microphone up to Anthony Stone's mouth.

"I wouldn't say that,"

"This is the third victim in two months, how can you or the police department assure us that we will be safe with a serial killer out here chopping up his victims left and right?" Another reporter asked.

"The only thing I can assure you is that I will catch this guy," Anthony Stone pushed through the crowd, slid behind the wheel of his all black Dodge Charger, and drove away from the crime scene in a hurry. Images of the last victims chopped up body played over and over again in his head. When Anthony Stone left the crime scene, he knew right then and there that he was going to have to personally take down the so-called Uncle Sam.

Anthony Stone pulled up in front of his apartment building, killed the engine, and headed inside. It had been a long day and all he wanted to do was relax and have a drink. Anthony Stone entered his apartment and quickly pulled out his 9mm when he heard movement coming from the kitchen area. He eased his way towards the kitchen and aimed his gun at the intruder.

"Oh my god!" Tasha said holding her heart. "You trying to give me a heart attack or something?"

"Tasha what are you doing here?" Anthony Stone said holstering his weapon.

"Sorry I was just trying to surprise you with dinner," She said innocently. "I saw you on the news, and it looked like you were having a bad day so I figured that you could use a nice home cooked meal along with some company."

Anthony Stone shook his head. "I almost shot you," he had given Tasha the keys to his apartment over two months ago, but since she never used them he had forgotten that she even had them. He was taking his time with this relationship, it seemed like every time he found someone he really liked, and his job would somehow get in the way or ruin the relationship. But not this time, this time he planned to take his time and make sure that Tasha was the right one for him. Anthony Stone leaned in and kissed Tasha on the lips. "It smells good baby, what you cooking?"

"It's a surprise," Tasha smiled, and then pushed her man out of the kitchen when she caught him trying to peek inside one of the pots. Tasha stood at 5"7 with jet-black hair that came down to the middle of her back. Her skin complexion was a shade darker than caramel. She favored the actor Nia Long. Tasha weighed 180 lbs. and carried it well.

Anthony Stone sat on the couch as Fabolous new album hummed through the speakers on the entertainment system. He poured himself a glass of vodka and mixed it with orange juice. The drink was just what he needed to calm his nerves. Twenty minutes later, Tasha emerged from the kitchen and placed two plates down on the kitchen table.

Anthony Stone made his way over to the table, as he and Tasha held hands while he said a quick prayer over the food. Once that was done the two dug in.

"This ain't bad," Anthony Stone said.

"I used my grandmother's recipe," Tasha smiled. This was her first time making lamb chops and she was hoping that Anthony liked them. As Tasha ate her food she noticed that Anthony was drinking a lot and seemed to have a lot on his mind, she had been watching the news so she knew what was going on. "Want to talk about it?"

"Sorry baby," Stone apologized. "I don't know how someone could kill a person and then chop their body up like it's nothing, images of that woman's body keep popping up in my head."

Tasha walk around to the other side of the table and rubbed Anthony Stone's back. "It's going to be okay, I'm sure they'll catch him sooner or later.

"I got assigned to the case tonight baby," he announced. He knew that Tasha would be upset because that meant longer hours and less time that they would be able to spend together.

"I understand," Tasha rubbed his back. "If anybody can catch him it's you," she didn't like the idea of him having to track down a serial killer, but that was his job and it was her job to support him.

"Thank you baby," Anthony Stone kissed, Tasha on the cheek, walked over to the couch and fired up his laptop. He was determined to find out who this Uncle Sam guy was. He knew the faster he found out who the man was, the faster he would be able to stop the murders.

48 HƐURS TO DIE

CHAPTER 2

"It's Not Safe"

Uncle Sam sat upstairs in the office of the club that he owned watching CNN. He grinned when he heard the reporter announce that the police had no leads on who the suspect was. Reggie ran a successful nightclub as well as a few other lucrative businesses by day, but by night, he turned from Reggie the businessman to Uncle Sam the serial killer. Reggie began his killings about six months ago when his fiancé at the time was murdered in a hostage situation. The detective on duty the night that his fiancé was murdered was none other than Anthony Stone. Reggie remembered the detective apologizing for not being able to save his fiancé, but he paid the detective no mind, in his heart he felt that detective Stone along with the rest of the police department could have done way more but they chose not to. From that day forth, Reggie planned to make the police do their jobs. He planned to kill as many people as he had to in order to make his point. Reggie's victims were all women, the police had failed to protect his woman, and now he wanted to see just how many women had to die in order for them to finally start doing what they were being paid to do, protect and serve.

Reggie exited his office, stood out on the balcony area, and looked down at all the people on the dance floor. The club was packed wall-to-wall with partygoers dancing, drinking, and having a good time. The sad part was that one of them was going to be Uncle Sam's next victim and they didn't even have a clue.

Reggie sipped his drink when he heard a knock at the door; he turned around and saw Lisa standing in the doorway. He had hired Lisa to manage the club and to basically do all the work that he was supposed to be doing or too lazy to do. Lisa was a Latin woman who had a great personality, not to mention she was easy on the eyes, with a nice coke bottle figure.

"Numbers are looking real good tonight," Lisa smiled. "We got a full house tonight, with plenty of people outside dying to get inside."

Reggie sipped his drink and nodded. "You've been doing a phenomenal job keep it up."

"Thank you," Lisa said with a smile. She had been working with Reggie for over a year and she still wasn't able to read him. Reggie never said more than necessary and seemed to be strictly all about business. Lisa had even asked to take Reggie out on a date a few time, but he always declined. "Is everything alright? Seems like something is on your mind."

"I'm good, Lisa thank you," Reggie sipped his drink. "Close the door on your way out," he dismissed her. Lisa was a good worker and a good friend, but Reggie refused to let the people who he worked with into his world, just In case the cops ever came around asking question they would have nothing but good things to say about him. The less they knew the better.

Reggie looked down at the crowd when he noticed a blonde haired woman throw up on the bar. Immediately two of his bouncers escorting the woman out of the club. Each bouncer was given specific orders to throw out anyone who couldn't control their alcohol and women were no exception.

Reggie grabbed his suit jacket and headed for the exit. Usually he never shits where he eats, but tonight he just couldn't let the drunk blonde slip through the cracks. He exited his office and trotted downstairs to where Lisa stood talking to one of the club promoters "Something just came up. I have to go, I'll call you in the morning," he told, Lisa when he made it downstairs then quickly made his exit.

48 HƎURS TO DIE

CHAPTER 3

"Don't Do It"

The lady with the blonde hair only made it a couple of blocks away from the club before she was throwing up again. She ran in between two parked cars and let it out in a painful sounding heap. The cocaine, alcohol, and heat all combined wasn't a good mixture for the young lady. She sat down on the curb trying to gather her thoughts and take in some fresh air when a black 911 Porsche pulled up to a stop directly in front of her. The blonde woman eyed the fancy car hoping it may of been someone she knew, but the tint were so dark she couldn't see inside the car.

The woman spit on the ground when the passenger window to the Porsche slowly rolled down. "You alright?" The driver asked.

"Do I look okay?" Blonde slurred with an attitude.

"It's late why don't you let me give you a ride home," the driver offered.

"Fuck off asshole," she waved the driver off. She figured he was just some rich creep looking to have easy sex with her because she was drunk.

"You're in no condition to be out here by yourself," the driver pressed. "I'll give you a ride home free of charge."

Blonde was just about to curse the driver out when all of a sudden it began to pour down raining out of nowhere. Within five second, she was drenched. Blonde quickly hopped up off the curb and hopped in the passenger seat of the Porsche.

"Reggie," the driver held out his hand.

"Melissa," blonde shook his hand, as the Porsche pulled away from the curb in a hurry.

"Hungry?"

"Not really I just want to go home and get some rest," Melissa said with a slight attitude. "Can you believe those assholes at the club kicked me out?"

"Really?" Reggie asked faking ignorance. "Why did they do that?"

"Because I threw up one time," she fumed. "One bottle of water and I would of been fine,"

"There's another party going on tonight over on the west side if you're interested," Reggie threw it out there hoping that Melissa would take the bait.

Melissa sucked her teeth. "Dude I'm covered in throw up, I'm not going nowhere like this," she huffed. "What are you some kind of weirdo or something?"

"I understand," Reggie said as he drove. He tolerated Melissa's disrespect because he knew the payoff was going to be great. "Your address?" He turned and looked at, Melissa. He pretended to punch her address in the GPS as she slurred it out.

Fifteen minutes into the drive, Reggie looked over and saw that, Melissa was knocked out cold. All he could do was shake his head at her stupidity. Ten minutes later, he pulled up to his mansion and killed the engine. He turned and shook Melissa until she stirred awake.

"Where are we?" Melissa asked in a dry voice.

"I had to stop by the house real quick to grab something," Reggie told her. "I'll only be a second."

Melissa stepped out the Porsche and stretched her legs. "This your house?"

Reggie nodded. "Sure is."

Melissa's eyes went from the big house to the expensive suit that Reggie had on. "So what are you like some rich Wall street geek or something?"

Reggie opened the front door and ignored Melissa's last question. He'd had about enough of her mouth. "Make yourself at home I just have to grab something from upstairs. I'll be right back," he said before disappearing around the corner.

Melissa walked over towards the kitchen and opened the refrigerator. She grabbed a bottle of water and a bowl of grapes. She tossed grapes in her mouth one by one, as she nosily walked around the mansion looking for anything that she could steal. Melissa stood looking at a picture on the wall of Reggie with an NBA basketball player when she heard movement behind her, she spun around and saw Reggie standing there wearing a blue mechanic jumpsuit, his hands were slipped into a pair of latex gloves and he held a baseball bat by his side.

"What are you doing?" Melissa asked with a confused looked on her face. Without warning, Reggie swung the baseball bat with so much force that it could be heard cutting through the air until it make contact with Melissa's skull.

CRACK!

Reggie smiled as he watched Melissa's unconscious body laying at his feet. He whistled tunelessly as he picked Melissa up and her tossed her body over his shoulder and carried her downstairs to his basement. He violently tossed Melissa's body down to the basement floor. When Reggie had first began his killing streak he did it with hopes of teaching the police a lesson, but the more he killed the more he began to enjoy it. Reggie walked over to the closet and removed an ax. He stood over Melissa and shook his head with a disgusted look on his face. Reggie raised the ax over his head and brought it down with authority. He swung the ax repeatedly until his arms finally got tired. Reggie looked around and saw blood everywhere along with several of Melissa's body parts scattered across the floor. "See what you made me do," he whispered to Melissa's head that was over in a corner detached from her body.

48 HĪURS TO DIE

CHAPTER 4

"Surprise Surprise"

Anthony Stone pulled up to the crime scene and immediately he could see a crowd of people pooled on the sidewalk with their cell phones out recording and taking photos. He pushed his way through the crowd of bystanders and several members of the media. There were two cruisers and an ambulance parked out front. "Get this street roped off right now!" Anthony Stone yelled to one of the officers. He walked up to the other officer who had a look on his face as if he had just threw up.

"What do we have here?"

"A woman was walking past this car and noticed some type of red liquid leaking from the trunk and called us," The officer said. "Me and my partner popped the trunk and found this."

Anthony Stone approached the car, peaked inside the trunk, and immediately covered his nose. Inside the trunk looked to be chopped up body parts of a woman. "I want someone to dust this entire car for prints," he said as he slipped on a pair of latex gloves. The horrible scene inside of the trunk was enough to make anybody sick to their stomach. Anthony Stone looked around the trunk when he noticed an envelope with the number four written across it. He grabbed the envelope and found a letter inside.

"If you're reading this, then that means that once again the police weren't able to protect and serve the innocent. I wonder how many innocent people will have to die before the pigs finally start to do their jobs. We'll soon find out because I'm just getting started.

Sincerely yours: Uncle Sam."

Anthony Stone read the letter and immediately felt a fire burning inside his stomach. He badly wanted to catch this creep and teach him a lesson. He wondered what type of monster could do something like this to another human being, and more importantly, why?

Anthony Stone walked up to the uniform officer. "Any witnesses?"

"Nope," the officer shook his head. "It looks as if the body has been sitting here for almost twelve hours."

Anthony Stone felt his phone vibrating on his hip, he looked down at his screen and saw Captain Fisher's name flashing across the screen, and he quickly stepped away from the scene and answered. "Hey Captain,"

"I need you down at the station ASAP we got the victims roommate here," Captain Fisher said hanging up in Anthony Stone's ear.

48 HₓURS TO DIE

CHAPTER 5

"Questions"

Anthony Stone stepped foot inside the precinct and headed straight for Captain Fisher's office, before he even got a chance to knock, a strong voice on the other side of the door yelled, "Come in!"

Anthony Stone stepped inside the office and saw Captain Fisher sitting behind his desk with a cup of coffee in front of him. Over to his left, Anthony Stone spotted women with her face buried in her hands sniffling.

"Detective Stone, I'd like you to meet Tiffany," Captain Fisher turned to face Tiffany. "Hey Tiffany this here is the detective that I was telling you about, he's going to help find the guy who did this to your friend," Captain Fisher stood to his feet. "I'll leave you two alone," he said then exited the office.

"Here you go," Anthony Stone said as he sat on the edge of the desk and held out a tissue.

Tiffany looked up, and grabbed the tissue. "My friend didn't deserve this," she paused to blow her nose. "She was a sweet girl."

"You and the victim were roommates?"

"Yes."

"How long did ya'll live together for?" Anthony Stone pulled out his pad and began writing.

"Two years," Tiffany sobbed. "Melissa wouldn't hurt a fly."

"Did Melissa have any enemies?"

"None everybody loved Melissa."

"When was the last time you saw, Melissa alive?" Anthony Stone asked.

"Last night," Tiffany replied. "We went out to the club to celebrate my birthday."

"How did you two get separated in the club?" Anthony Stone asked scribbling down everything that Tiffany told him.

"The club was so crowded it was like she was standing right next to me one second, then the next she was gone," Tiffany wiped her eyes. "And that's the last time I saw her."

"Well then that means that her killer was more than likely inside that club," Anthony Stone said out loud. "What's the name of the club?"

"Club Blaze," Tiffany answered. "Ever heard of that club before?"

"Yes I'm familiar with Club Blaze," Anthony Stone replied. He had heard a lot about Club Blaze, it was the place where the big named celebrities partied when they were in town. Word on the streets was that Cub Blaze was one of the hardest clubs to get into. "Here's my card," he handed it to Tiffany. "If you hear or remember anything else give me a call."

Anthony Stone left the precinct and headed straight for Club Blaze. He had never been inside the club before but he planned on making an exception tonight.

***

Anthony Stone pulled up In front of the club and the front was crowded as if there were a concert going on inside. Women were lined all up and down the streets dressed in there skimpiest outfits trying to catch the eyes of the rich and famous. The few police officers that were present on the scene did their best to control the crowd that seemed to be growing by the minute. Anthony Stone stepped out of his vehicle and headed towards the entrance of the club. As he walked, he noticed twelve to fifteen foreign cars lined up back-to-back.

Anthony Stone reached the entrance and was met by a huge bouncer. "I need to speak with Reggie Braxton," he flashed his badge. The bouncer eyed the badge for a few seconds before allowing the detective access inside the club. Anthony Stone entered the club and immediately the loud bass from the speakers slapped him in the face. He squeezed through the crowded club and passed partygoers that danced wildly and others who were basically making love on the dance floor with their clothes on. Anthony Stone made his way over to a bouncer that looked over the crowd. "Where can I find the owner?" He yelled over the blaring music flashing his badge. The bounced eyed the badge suspiciously then said. "Wait right here!"

Anthony Stone stood over in the cut checking out the scenery when he felt a light tap on his shoulder. He spun around and saw an attractive Latin woman standing in front of him.

"May I help you?" The woman asked.

"Yes I need to speak with the owner of this place,"

"About?"

"I'm sorry who are you again?" Anthony Stone asked.

"I'm Lisa the manager of this place and Mr. Braxton's assistant."

"My name is detective Anthony Stone and either I speak to Mr. Braxton or I shut this place down you choose?" He was tired of playing word games with the woman.

Lisa smiled. "One second detective," she said then disappeared in the mist of the crowd.

48 HŎURS TO DIE

CHAPTER 6

"Business"

Reggie sat in his office watching CNN. He loved to hear about his crimes on the news, and he loved even more when they acknowledged that they had no clues or leads. Reggie sat up in his chair when he saw Anthony Stone on his TV screen and turned up the volume.

"Detective Stone, does your department have any clue who's behind these murders and is this now a serial matter?" A reporter asked.

"No comment," Anthony Stone replied as he pushed his way through the reporters.

"Do you have anything to say to the people?" Another reporter asked shoving his recorder up towards Anthony Stone's mouth.

Anthony Stone looked directly into the camera. "Yes I want to say to the person or people responsible for these murders I'm going to find you," he said with a smirk.

Reggie laughed as he sat back in his expensive chair. He thought it was funny for the detective to make a promise like that, a promise that he knew he would not be able to keep. A strong knock on his office door grabbed his attention. Reggie stood from his chair, walked over, and opened the door.

"There's a detective here saying that he needs to see you," Lisa said with a worried look on her face.

"Does he have a warrant?"

"I don't think so," Lisa answered.

"Did he say what he wanted?" Reggie asked.

"No all he said was that his name was Detective Anthony Stone," Lisa said.

Reggie smiled. "Send him up."

"Yes sir," Lisa turned and exited the office.

Reggie sat behind his desk and poured himself a drink as he awaited the arrival of Detective Stone.

48 HEURS TO DIE

CHAPTER 7

"Nice To See You Again"

"Detective Stone, have a seat," Reggie smiled as he stepped to side so the detective could enter his office.

"How you doing today Mr. Braxton?"

"You can call me Reggie," he smiled. "By the way it's nice to see you again detective."

"I'm sorry, have we met?" Anthony Stone asked.

"Once upon a time, but that's not important how can I help you tonight?" The fact that Detective Stone didn't remember him pissed Reggie off even more.

"Do you know this girl?" Anthony Stone asked handing Reggie a picture of Melissa. Reggie glanced at the picture for a second then handed back.

"I'm sorry I can't say that I do," Reggie sat back in his chair.

"She was murdered last night and last seen here in your club," Anthony Stone said.

"I'm sorry detective but I don't know every single person that enters my club," he said with a straight face.

"I'm sure you don't, but maybe one of your bouncers may have remembered a woman throwing up or saw her getting into a stranger's car or something."

"Are you saying that I or somebody on my staff is Uncle Sam, the serial killer?" Reggie asked with a raised brow.

"I never said that," Anthony Stone countered quickly. "Why are you getting so defensive?"

"Detective if I was getting defensive I would have told you I'm not speaking to you without my lawyer present," Reggie took a sip from his drink. "What I am saying is I'm not responsible for everybody that steps foot in my club, it's not my fault if they can't hold their liquor, or if they drink too much and end up going home with the wrong person, nothing I can do about that detective."

"But you are responsible for helping me with my investigation," Anthony Stone said. "Why wouldn't you want to help me catch Uncle Sam?"

"Help you catch Uncle Sam?" Reggie echoed. "I don't see you helping me fill this club up every night, but you expect me to help you do your job?" Reggie shook his head with a disgusted look on his face. "Are we done here detective? If so you can let yourself out."

Anthony Stone wanted to bash Reggie's face in, but instead he stood and left. He had more important things to do then to sit there and argue with an arrogant, rich asshole like Reggie.

Reggie stood on the balcony in his club and watched Anthony Stone's every move until he had finally exited the club. He had fun toying with the detective especially since he knew that the authorities had no clue who Uncle Sam was. Little did Anthony Stone know but this had just became personal. "Uncle Sam is about to make your life a living hell detective," Reggie said with an evil look in his eyes.

48 H3URS TO DIE

CHAPTER 8

"How Could You"

Anthony Stone entered his apartment and heard soft music. He walked further into the apartment and saw candles lit all around the apartment. He made his way to the dining room area and saw, Tasha sitting at the table all dressed up with a frown on her face. "Hey baby."

"Don't you hey baby me?" Tasha snapped. "You were supposed to be here three hours ago! You could have at least had the decency to call and say that you were going to be late!" Tasha stood to her feet and began blowing out all of the candles that laid around the apartment. It was Tasha's birthday and Anthony Stone had promised her a romantic dinner, but as usual, he was too busy consumed with work.

"I'm sorry baby," Anthony Stone began. "I was going to call but..."

Tasha tossed a glass against the wall. "Don't lie to me Anthony; you totally forgot all about me and my birthday. All you care about is your stupid job!"

"Baby calm down," Anthony Stone said. "My job is to protect and keep people safe if I don't do my job then..."

"Protect our relationship and keep my heart safe how about that!" Tasha countered. "I'm not competing with your job!"

Anthony Stone went to grab, Tasha's wrist so she wouldn't walk away from him, but she quickly jerked her arm free from his grip and slapped him across the face.

"Don't you ever touch me again?" She said out of anger. She couldn't believe that he had totally forgotten about her birthday, and what made it worst was that he didn't even have the decency to call and say he wouldn't be able to make it. "You got me sitting here in the dark with candles lit looking like a fool!" Tasha turned to slap Anthony Stone again, but this time he caught her wrist in mid swing.

"That's enough!" He growled through clenched teeth. "You need to go in the bedroom and cool off."

"Get your hands off me!" Tasha jerked her hand out of Anthony's grip. "I'm leaving," she said and stormed off towards the bedroom. Tasha stopped when she reached the bedroom door and looked back at Anthony Stone. "And since you love your job so much, maybe you can make love to that tonight," she stormed into the bedroom and slammed the door so hard that one Anthony Stone's trophies that sat on the wall unit fell over.

Anthony Stone sighed loudly as he flopped down on the couch. He didn't mean to forget about Tasha's birthday, but the brutal murders by the hands of Uncle Sam was enough to take over anyone's mind. He understood why Tasha was mad, any woman would have been mad if the man they loved had forgotten about their birthday. The truth was he didn't forget about Tasha's birthday, he had just lost track of time.

Anthony Stone stood to his feet and was about to go and check on Tasha when he heard a knock at the front door. He wondered who could have been knocking at his door since he rarely ever had company drop by. Anthony Stone looked through the peephole and didn't see anyone standing on the other side of the door. He slowly opened the door with caution and stuck his head out into the hallway. Anthony Stone looked back and forth. Empty. The hallway was completely empty. "That was strange," Anthony Stone said to himself, he closed the door and saw

Tasha exiting the bedroom with a duffle bag in her hand. "Where are you going?"

"Home!" Tasha said with an attitude. It was going to take some time for her to forgive him for this.

"Baby can we talk about this please?" Anthony Stone said blocking Tasha's path so she couldn't leave. He loved Tasha with all her heart and the last thing he wanted was for her to leave.

"We don't have nothing else to talk about!" Tasha snapped. Anthony Stone went to respond when out of nowhere he heard loud banging on his front door.

BANG!

BANG!

BANG!

Anthony Stone whipped his gun out of his holster with a snap. "Go back into the bedroom and don't come out until I tell you to," he waited until Tasha was in the bedroom safe and sound before he made his way towards the front door. Anthony Stone snatched the door open and stepped out into the hallway. Again, it was empty. He held a two handed grip on his 9mm as he inched his way down the hall towards the staircase. He snatched the staircase door open and saw a figure in all black jetting up the stairs heading towards the next level.

"Hey stop!" Anthony Stone yelled. The man in all black quickly turned and fired two reckless shots over his shoulder as he continued up the stairs at a fast pace. Without thinking twice, Anthony Stone took off after the gunman. He ran up the stairs skipping two at a time until he heard the staircase door open and close on the floor above him. Anthony Stone cautiously inched his way up to the next level and snatched the door open. With a two handed grip on his 9mm he stepped out into the hallway. An apartment door opened and an older woman stuck her head.

"What the hell is going on out here?" She asked nosily.

"Ma'am go back into your apartment!" Anthony Stone yelled as he continued on down the hall.

"I'm calling the police," the old lady said stepping back inside her apartment.

Anthony Stone eased his way down the hallway when another apartment door swung open from behind him. He spun around just as the gunman dressed in all black sprang from the apartment and tackled Anthony Stone down to the floor. The gun accidentally discharged as the two men went crashing down to the floor. The gunman bent Anthony Stone's wrist backwards forcing him to release his grip on the firearm. Anthony Stone quickly hopped up to his feet and took a fighting stance. There was no way he was going to let the gunman escape. Anthony Stone moved in and threw a hook, the gunman ducked the punch easily and scooped Anthony Stone's legs from up under him and dumped him on his head. The gunman quickly got on top of Anthony Stone and delivered a vicious combination of punches and elbows. Anthony Stone bucked his mid-section wildly and got the gunman off of him. He crawled back to his feet but the gunman was on him. The gunman grab the back of Anthony Stone's head and delivered a knee to the detective's rib cage, then followed up with a sharp hook to Anthony Stone's temple. It was obvious that the gunman had some mixed martial arts skills. Having no other choice Anthony Stone rushed the gunman and tried to tackle him down to the floor, but the gunman used his momentum against him and slung the detectives head first into the wall. All the commotion had caused several tenants to nosily stick their heads out their doors to see what was going on. Anthony Stone dove down to the floor and grabbed his 9mm; he aimed it at the gunman's departing back but didn't pull the trigger. There were too many innocent by standers standing in the hallway being nosey. "Damn!" Anthony Stone yelled as he quickly hopped up to his feet and ran after the gunman. He reached the staircase and stopped. He had no clue if the gunman had ran upstairs or downstairs.

"Damn!"

48 HƎURS TO DIE

CHAPTER 9

"Missed Opportunity"

Anthony Stone sat on the couch in his apartment as a paramedic tended to the small cut that was right above his eye. His entire apartment building was now crawling with police.

"Are you okay baby?" Tasha asked with a worried look on her face. After everything that had happened, she felt stupid for starting an argument over something so small.

She now realized how serious her man's job really was and why he had to spend so many hours away from home, it took something like this to happen for it all to start to make sense to Tasha.

"I'm good baby but I'm going to need you to go stay at your mother's house until I get to the bottom of this situation," Anthony Stone told her. There was no way he planned on letting Tasha stay in his apartment especially after what had just happened.

"How long will I have to stay over there?" Tasha asked with a disappointed look on her face.

"Not sure," Anthony Stone said honestly. He still didn't have a clue how the gunman had found out where he lived. That was something that was going to bother him until he figured it out.

"Did you get a look at the guys face?" Tasha asked.

Anthony Stone shook his head as he noticed, Captain Fisher enter his apartment.

"You alright?" Captain Fisher asked.

"I'm still alive," Anthony Stone chuckled.

"Looks like you have a fan," Captain Fisher smiled. "This should get interesting,"

"Detective?" A uniform officer said entering the apartment, in his hand he held an envelope. "I found this out in the hallway," he held the envelope out towards detective Stone. Anthony Stone grabbed the envelope and saw that the envelope had his name written on it. He opened the envelope and began reading.

"I heard you were out here looking for me, so I figured I'd make your job easier. The next time we meet, I'll make sure I'll bring my brand new ax with me. I spared you tonight, the next time I won't be so generous. Oh and by the way, tell Tasha I said happy birthday.

Yours truly: Uncle Sam"

"I'm going to kill him!" Anthony Stone growled as he handed, Captain Fisher the letter so he could read it.

"Is everything okay baby?" Tasha asked with a nervous look on her face.

"Yes everything is fine," Anthony Stone said quickly, and then turned to face the uniform officer. "You mind taking her to her mother's house?" There was no way he was going to tell, Tasha what was in that note.

"No problem at all sir," the officer replied.

"Also, I want a patrol car outside of her mother's house twenty fours a day and seven days a week," Anthony Stone ordered, then turned and faced, Tasha. "Go with this officer and I'll call you in a little while, and I'm sorry again about your birthday," he apologized.

"It's okay baby, I love you,"

"Love you too baby," Anthony Stone said as he watched Tasha exit the apartment with the officer.

"Stone I know you are upset but you still have to think with a clear head here," Captain Fisher reminded him.

"When people go off emotions that's when they usually make mistakes."

Anthony Stone nodded his head. "You're right," What really bothered him was how Uncle Sam had figured out where he lived and had gotten so close to him.

48 H⌛URS TO DIE

CHAPTER 10

"Serious Business"

Reggie sat behind the wheel of his vehicle parked two blocks away from Anthony Stone's apartment. He enjoyed toying with the detective, and was just getting started. Reggie watched closely as a uniform officer escorted Anthony Stone's girlfriend in the front seat of his squad car. Reggie chuckled at how sloppy the police were. "This is going to be easier than I expected," he smiled as he pulled off and tailed the squad car. Reggie planned on turning detective Stone's life upside down. He followed the squad car to a plain looking house. Reggie quickly pulled out a note pad and scribbled down the address. "Got you," he smiled.

48 H⏳URS TO DIE

CHAPTER 11

"Catch Me If You Can"

The next day, Anthony Stone sat at his desk stuck in his own thoughts. He still couldn't believe that Uncle Sam had actually shown up at his home and violated his personal space. Anthony Stone had decided to still remain in his apartment in hopes that the serial killer tried his luck again. There was no way he was going to let someone run him out of his home. What really bothered

Anthony Stone was how shaken up Tasha was. She was trying to be strong, but Anthony Stone could tell that the situation had really shook her up.

Anthony Stone sipped on his coffee when he felt his phone buzzing on his hip. He looked down at his screen and saw that whoever was calling him had took the time to block their number. "Hello?" He answered.

"Hello detective."

Immediately, Anthony Stone waved and got another detective's attention, then gave him a hand signal to trace the call. "Uncle Sam?"

"The one and only," the caller said arrogantly.

"I was expecting your call," Anthony Stone began. "We have some unfinished business to discuss why don't you come on down to the precinct so we can talk."

Uncle Sam chuckled. "Sorry but my hands are a little full at the moment," right then and there Anthony Stone heard a muffled scream in the background. "I'm sitting here with a beautiful young woman named Mya, in exactly twenty minutes I'm going to cut her open like a fish!"

"Listen Uncle Sam, that won't be necessary," Anthony Stone said trying to buy himself some extra time as several detective's and officers surrounded his desk and listened on through his speakerphone. "Tell me where you and I'll trade my life for the girl. Let the girl go and take me instead," he offered.

"I just emailed the address to where she is, if you're not here in twenty minutes the girl dies!" Uncle Sam said in a calm tone, and then hung up in the detective's ear.

"Shit!" Anthony Stone cursed as he quickly checked his email, and just as Uncle Sam promised there as an address in his inbox. "We have to move now that address is about twenty minutes from here!" He said which meant he didn't have much time He quickly rushed outside to his car. Anthony Stone pulled out of his parking spot like a mad man. The last thing he wanted was another dead body on his watch, whoever this Uncle Sam guy was, he was really starting to become a pain in the behind. Anthony Stone zoomed through the streets jumping from lane to lane, time was running out, and he knew it.

48 HZURS TO DIE

CHAPTER 12

"Out Of Time"

Anthony Stone pulled up in front of the address and glanced down at his watch. Twenty-two minutes had passed since the phone call with Uncle Sam. Anthony Stone hopped out of his car and sprinted towards the front door of the house. He removed his 9mm, and noticed that the front door was left slightly ajar. He eased the door open and slowly stepped inside the house as the sound of loud sirens could be heard just outside the door. As Anthony

Stone eased his way through the house, he noticed a trail of blood leading towards the back room. He reached the back room, paused, then came forward, and kicked the room door open. Inside the room, Anthony Stone found a woman's body parts chopped up and thrown all around the room. Over on the window seal he spotted an envelope with the number five written on it in blood. Anthony Stone opened the envelope and began to read the letter.

"If you're reading this then that means you ran out of time. Another woman is dead because of the police, what is it going to take for the police to start doing their job the proper way? I guess you pigs like doing things the hard way. That's cool with me because I'm just getting warmed up.

Sincerely yours: Uncle Sam."

Anthony Stone tossed the letter down to the floor and exited the room. This serial killer was really beginning to piss him off. The apartment was now flooded with officers and EMT workers.

"Detective!" An officer called out getting, Anthony Stone's attention. "This blood is still warm; it's possible that our killer may still be close by."

Anthony Stone nodded, and then exited the apartment. He needed some fresh air and to clear his mind. He stepped outside and the first thing he spotted was a huge crowd standing behind the crime tape. Right now, he could really use a drink. Uncle Sam was toying with him and making him look like a fool. Anthony Stone noticed the media pull up to the scene when he felt his cell phone vibrating on his hip. He looked down at the screen and saw that the number was private. "Yeah," he answered.

"Ran out of time I see," Uncle Sam chuckled.

"Why are you doing this?"

"Because I can," Uncle Sam countered. "It's sad that I have to go to this extreme to get you pigs to do your job."

"That's no excuse for what you're doing!" Anthony Stone snapped. "Meet me one on one like a man and let's settle this."

"Detective, you don't look too good," Uncle Sam chuckled. "And aren't those the same clothes you had on last night?"

"You're watching me?" Anthony Stone asked as the line suddenly went dead. He quickly looked out into the crowd of people that stood behind the crime scene tape.

"Detective is this the work of the same serial killer?" A reporter asked shoving a microphone in Anthony Stone's face. Anthony Stone ignored the reporter as he searched the sea of faces that flooded the sidewalk.

"Detective Stone can you tell us what happened here tonight?" Another reporter asked. Anthony Stone ignored the question and continued to look out into the crowd. Anthony Stone stopped when he locked eyes with a man standing across the street dressed in all black with a black hoodie on his head with the strings drawn tight making it hard to see his entire face. When the two made eye contact the hooded man quickly turned and began to walk off.

"Detective Stone do you have anything to say to the people?" A reporter asked. Anthony Stone tuned the reporter out as he slowly began to follow the hooded man down the street. He wasn't sure if the hooded man was Uncle Sam or not, but his gut was telling him that the hooded man was indeed the man he was looking for. As Anthony Stone followed the hooded man, a downpour of rain suddenly began to fall from the sky. Anthony Stone pulled his 9mm from his holster and held it down by his side, as he walked not wanting to scare any innocent bystanders that may have been lingering around. He quickened up his pace and when he was in a close enough distance he yelled, "Freeze!"

As soon as the words left Anthony Stone's lips, the hooded man took off in a sprint.

The hooded man took off in a sprint when the detective yelled freeze. He pulled a .45 off his waistline and fired two shots over his shoulder. He was willing to do whatever he had to in order to escape with his life and his freedom. The hooded man ran out into the street and nearly got side swiped by a car. Several car horns sounded loudly as the hooded ran through the intersection. Right before the hooded man reached the other side of the street a Honda came to a screeching stop. The driver stepped on the brakes a little too late as he watched the hooded man smash into his windshield, his momentum carrying him over the roof of the Honda and sent him crashing down on the concrete. The hooded man hit the concrete hard, looked up, and saw a Mack truck headed right for him. The driver of the Mack truck stomped down on the brakes as soon as he saw the man standing. The hooded man watched as the grill on the Mack truck stopped one inch away from his face. The hooded man hopped up off the ground with the quickness and took off running again.

48 HΞURS TO DIE

CHAPTER 13

"Run For Your Life"

Anthony Stone crossed the intersection and lost the hooded man that quick. He looked left and right, but saw nothing. He knew the hooded man couldn't have gotten that far. When the hooded man fired off those two shots, it forced Anthony Stone to take cover behind a parked car.

The driver of the Mack stepped out of the truck and approached the detective.

"Looking for a man in a black hooded sweat shirt did you happen to see which way he went?" Anthony Stone asked.

"I almost hit him with my truck, god must have been on his side," the truck driver said. "He came out of where I almost didn't..."

"Shh!" Anthony Stone said as he shined his light up into the woods. That's when he heard it again, someone was moving through the woods, breaking twigs, and stepping on dry, crunchy leaves. Anthony Stone took off into the woods after the hooded man. Anthony Stone held his flashlight just above his 9mm as he eased his way through the woods. He took slow, cautious steps not wanting to attract attention to his location. Anthony Stone waved his flashlight from left to right as he moved out deeper into the woods. He took his left hand and turned down the volume on his walkie-talkie so it wouldn't give up his location. He continued to inch through the woods when a chunk of the tree he stood next to exploded. Anthony Stone quickly ducked down. He had no clue where the hooded man was, the dark woods made it hard for him to see. Anthony Stone pointed his flashlight in the direction that the shot came from but saw nothing. Then suddenly he heard footsteps coming from his left. Anthony Stone quickly aimed his gun in the direction of the footsteps, and opened fire.

POW!

POW!

POW!

POW!

Anthony Stone stood still for a second listening to see if he could pinpoint the hooded man's location. Seconds later, several shots were fired in the detective's direction followed by the sound of footsteps running in the opposite direction. Anthony Stone hopped up to take off after the hooded man but stopped when he felt a pain in his leg. He shined his flashlight down on his leg and saw blood. One of the hooded man bullets must have grazed his leg.

By the time Anthony Stone limped out of the woods, the hooded man was long gone. He cursed himself over and over again knowing how close he was to taking Uncle Sam off the streets.

Thirty minutes later, Anthony Stone noticed Captain Fisher heading in his direction while an EMT worker worked on his leg.

"Tell me you got a look at this guy's face," Captain Fisher asked.

Anthony Stone shook his head. "I was so close to catching this guy."

Captain Fisher patted, Anthony Stone on the back. "You'll get him next time champ. Go home and get you some rest."

Anthony Stone slid behind the wheel of his car and slowly pulled out into traffic. He still couldn't believe how close he had come to capturing Uncle Sam. He merged onto the highway when he heard cell phone ringing. Anthony Stone looked down at the screen and saw that the caller was calling from a private number. "Yeah," he answered.

"Close but no cigar," the caller laughed. "Detective Stone when are you going to realize that you're never going to catch me?"

"Never say never," Anthony Stone countered.

"I'll always be one step ahead of you detective," Uncle Sam chuckled.

"What kind of animal are you?" Anthony Stone yelled. "What type of real man gets turned on by harming innocent women?"

Uncle Sam chuckled again. "You just don't get it detective."

"If you're going to pick on someone at least pick on someone who'll defend themselves."

"Like who, Tasha?"

"If you even think about touching her I'll kill you!" Anthony Stone said with venom dripping from his tone. Before he could say another word, the line went dead. Without thinking twice, Anthony Stone stomped down on the gas. There was no way that he was going to allow Uncle Sam to harm Tasha. He would never be able to forgive himself if he allowed her to get hurt because of him. Anthony Stone pulled up to Tasha's mother's house and came to a screeching stop, hopped out with his 9mm already in his hand. Anthony Stone reached the front door and thought about kicking it in, but then decided to ring the doorbell instead. If nobody answered the door in ten seconds, Anthony Stone had already made up his mind that he was going to kick the door down. His reached a silent count of seven when finally; Tasha's mother answered the door.

"Hey Anthony," Ms. Brown said stepping to the side so that Anthony Stone could come inside. "Is everything alright?" She asked when she noticed his face covered in sweat and a gun in his hand.

"Sorry Ms. Brown," Anthony Stone apologized holstering his weapon. "I just wanted to make sure that you and Tasha were alright."

"Hey Anthony what are you doing here?" Tasha said coming from around the corner. "Are you okay?" She asked when she noticed that his forehead was covered in sweat.

"I got a call from Uncle Sam," Anthony Stone admitted. "I thought you and your mother may have been in danger."

"Baby he's playing with your mind," Tasha grabbed, Anthony Stone's hand and led him upstairs to her old bedroom. Once inside the bedroom Tasha closed the door, and made Anthony Stone lay down across her bed, she slowly removed his shirt and began to give him a strong-handed massage. "Don't let that creep serial killer get inside of your head baby," Tasha said in a soft whisper. "You are smarter than him, if he wants to play chess then you play chess with him, you can beat him,"

"I know baby, but this thing has gotten a little personal," he explained. "And the last thing I want is something to happen to you or your mother."

"There's an officer parked outside the front of the house at all times we'll be fine," Tasha told him. "Focus on catching this scum bag so we can go back to living a normal life, don't get me wrong I love my mother to death but I'm ready to go home."

"I'm on it baby," Anthony Stone rolled over onto his back and gave, Tasha a long slow kiss. "I love you and would die if something happened to you because of me."

Tasha chuckled, "Baby I'm fine, and I'm a big girl,"

"I know you are baby," Anthony Stone said. The truth was Tasha had no clue how dangerous Uncle Sam really was and he wasn't going to tell her the truth about how dangerous the serial killer really was because then she would be scared to death and that's the last thing he wanted. "I have to get going baby."

"No," Tasha wined. "Can you they with me tonight pleeeeease?" It had been a week since the couple had slept in the same bed together and Anthony Stone hated to admit it, but he missed, Tasha like crazy. For the rest of the night, Tasha laid her head on Anthony Stone's chest as the two watched "Martin" until they both fell asleep.

48 HEURS TO DIE

CHAPTER 14

"Now It's Personal"

Reggie sat in his office at the club with one leg crossed over the other and leaned back in his expensive chair. He didn't like how close Anthony Stone had come to catching him the other day. Things were getting too close so. Reggie decided to fall back and take a break for a minute and come up with a strategy that would surely ruin Anthony Stone's life, but at the same time, he had to be careful, knowing that one mistake could be the end of his life. Reggie watched CNN and the authorities still had no clue who or where Uncle Sam was. The club wasn't scheduled to open for the next four hours, but Reggie liked to sit in his office and think. Reggie sat looking up at the flat screen in his office when he heard a loud knock at the door.

"Come in!" He yelled. A second later in walked Lisa carrying two plastic bags. "Hey Lisa?" Reggie asked with a confused look on his face. When he dealt with his employees he made sure, he kept things strictly business.

"Hey," Lisa said with a huge smile on her face. "I saw you up here so I brought us some food from that new barbeque place down the street; I figured you may be hungry."

"Thanks Lisa I appreciate it," Reggie said with a smile. In his head, he was formulating a nice way to kick her out of his office without seeming rude.

"Mind if I join you?" Lisa asked pulling up a chair before, Reggie even got a chance to answer. "You never want to take me out on a date so I figured I'd bring the date to you. I promise I won't bite."

"Nothing personal but I just like to keep my business and my personal life separate," Reggie explained. "I would hate for things to get all messy you know?"

"I get it," Lisa said taking a bite out of her barbeque ribs. "But you're always cooped up in this office all the time, so I figured I'd come up here and hang out with you," she took another bite of her ribs. "So do you have a girlfriend, dating anyone, kids?"

Reggie took in a mouth full of mac and cheese. "No girlfriend, not dating anyone, and no kids, all I do is work. I'm too busy to have a personal life."

"Well I think we need to change that," Lisa said. "Change is good and you never know maybe I can be the one to spice up your life."

Reggie chuckled. "Spice is the last thing I need in my life right about now."

"You sure about that?" Lisa asked with a raised brow. "What if I told you that you weren't as innocent as you portray to be?"

"Excuse me?"

Lisa took another bite of her ribs. "What if I told you I followed you that night when you left the club early?"

"Huh," Reggie said with a confused look on his face.

"I saw you pick up the drunk girl what's her name? Melissa," Lisa smiled. "She was last seen with you, then the next day her body was found chopped up in little pieces," she bit down into her ribs again. "I know you murdered that girl."

Reggie let out a nervous laugh. "That's absurd."

"Is it really? Uncle Sam," she said letting it be known that she knew exactly who Reggie really was.

Reggie wiped his mouth and leaned back in his seat. "Okay Lisa what is it exactly that you want?"

"I want in," she smiled.

"I'm confused."

"You heard me I want in," Lisa repeated. "I want to help you kill."

Reggie took a close look at Lisa's face to see if she was serious. "How many people have you told about this?"

"I haven't told anyone about this...yet," she smiled. "Listen Reggie all I want to do is help."

Reggie wanted to tell Lisa that he worked alone, but he knew if he did that, she would more than likely try to blackmail him into letting her onboard. He wanted to slice her throat right there in his office but he couldn't because he had no clue if she had told anyone about his little secret. "Why are you doing this?"

"Listen Reggie I know you like me, but you've been keeping me away because of your little secret," Lisa smiled. "So now that we're partners I was thinking maybe we could go on a date tonight a real one."

It was at that moment when Reggie knew that Lisa had him by the balls. "Sure dinner sounds good to me."

"Great, meet me at my place tonight at 11 pm," Lisa smiled, spun, and made her exit leaving Reggie alone with his thoughts.

Reggie sat back in his chair with a frustrated look on his face. He had to think of a clever way to kill Lisa, but first he had to make sure that she didn't tell anyone about his little secret.

48 HƷURS TO DIE

CHAPTER 15

"A New Relationship"

R eggie pulled up in front of Lisa's house and killed the engine. He glanced down at his watch the time was 11:11 pm. He rang the doorbell and a few seconds later, Lisa answered the door wearing a pair of black fish net stockings and a black see through top. Lisa held a glass of wine in her hand. "I thought you may have gotten lost for a second," she smiled stepping to the side so Reggie could enter.

"You have a lovely home," Reggie said as Lisa led him over towards the dining room where he saw candles lit up all around the kitchen table. "All this for little ole me?"

"You know what they say," Lisa took a sip of her wine. "You only get one chance at a first impression."

Reggie removed his suit jacket and rested it on the back of his chair, and helped himself to a glass of wine. Lisa served ox tails, brown rice, and grilled mushrooms. "So what is it that you want from me?"

"I want to be your partner," Lisa answered quickly.

"How do I know that you're ready to take a life?" Reggie questioned.

"Test me."

"This isn't a game!" Reggie said his tone turning deadly. "Taking a life is not a game; I have a personal beef with the NYPD. I'm not just doing this for fun and games!"

"Let me help you teach the NYPD a lesson," Lisa begged. "I promise I'll be a wonderful protégé."

Reggie sat back, took a sip of his wine, and began thinking of ways that, Lisa could be of some use. At first, he didn't like the idea, but the more he thought about it the more he began to see the bigger picture of how he could use her to become the best and most famous serial killer of all time. "I have the perfect test for you, you pass this test, and then you can consider yourself my partner, deal?"

Lisa stood up, walked over towards Reggie, and straddled him. She leaned forward and kissed him on the lips. "Of course we have a deal."

While Lisa rested on Reggie's lap, he inhaled her perfume, and was immediately turned on. He hadn't been with women since his wife had been murdered and could no longer resist the urge. Reggie held Lisa by the waist, and stood to his feet. Lisa wrapped her legs around his waist, as the two passionately kissed while Reggie carried her to the bedroom.

After a long night of lovemaking, Reggie laid on the bed staring up at the ceiling while; Lisa snored lightly while her head rested on his chest. Reggie's mind was on ways he could kind of ease Lisa into the swing of things instead of throwing her straight into the fire. She had him stuck between a rock and a hard place. Now it was time for him to find a way to turn this situation into a win- win scenario. Reggie looked over and Lisa while she slept and wondered if she had what it took to take a life, wondered if she were able to keep her mouth shut afterwards. Reggie enjoyed working alone, but since a partner was being forced on him he now had to make some serious adjustments.

48 HĒURS TO DIE

CHAPTER 16

"The Next Day"

"You see that house right there?" Reggie sat behind the wheel of the stolen minivan and pointed towards an average looking single family home.

"Yeah what about it," Lisa spat.

"That's the house of our next victim," Reggie said with a no nonsense look on his face. "You ready to do this?"

"Hold on for a second," Lisa turned her gaze on, Reggie. "That lady lives in that house with her little two kids," she pointed out.

"And what's your point?" Reggie said coldly. "If I'm going to trust you, then I need to know that you can handle yourself under pressure."

"I can handle the pressure, but what about the kids?" Lisa asked.

"What about them?" Reggie said handing; Lisa a pistol with a silencer attached the barrel.

Lisa took the gun, exited the minivan, and slowly made her way towards the house of their latest victim. She took a deep breath and rang the doorbell. Seconds later, a blonde haired woman in her late thirties answered the door with a confused look on her face. "May I help you?"

Lisa didn't reply, instead she pulled out her pistol and put a bullet between the blonde haired woman's eyes. She watched as the woman's body collapsed. Lisa then entered the house, stood over the woman's body, and fired two more bullets into her body for good measures. Once that was done, Lisa made her way through the house in search of the two children. Lisa made her way upstairs and in the first room up ahead she spotted a young boy and girl that couldn't have been no older than eight sitting on a bed with a PlayStation controller in each of their hands. Lisa stepped in the room and snatched the plug to the TV out the wall quickly getting the children's attention. "On your feet!" She ordered as watched the kids do as they were told. Lisa escorted the two kids downstairs where, Reggie standing in the living room holding an ax in his hand. The children saw the man standing holding an ax and immediately busted out in tears.

Reggie looked over at, Lisa. "Shut those kids up now!"

Lisa aimed her gun at the little boy first. Her hand shook uncontrollably as her eyes began to water. "I can't do it," she lowered her gun.

Reggie walked up with a calm look on his face; he placed a friendly hand on, Lisa's shoulder. "It's okay."

"I'm sorry but this is a little too much for me," Lisa admitted.

"I understand," Reggie said. Without warning, he turn and swung the ax as if it was a baseball bat. Lisa looked on in horror as the little boy's head hit the wall then roll across the floor.

Reggie then turned his attention on the little girl. Lisa had to shut her eyes; she didn't have the heart nor the guts to take a child's life. She was beginning to realize that she might have been in a little over her head. Lisa sat in the kitchen trying to get her head together but was having a hard time doing that as she could still hear, Reggie in the other room chopping up the kids bodies. Lisa was thinking about jetting out the front door when, Reggie entered the kitchen covered in blood.

"What happen back there?"

Lisa wiped the tears from her face and took a deep a breath. "I'm sorry I wasn't ready for this tonight, maybe you should have started me off with something a little more easier."

"It's okay," Reggie said as he draped his arm around, Lisa's shoulder as they made her way back to the stolen minivan.

48 H𝓧URS TO DIE

CHAPTER 17

"Unbelievable"

Anthony Stone pulled up to the crime scene and from how many reporters and news vans were parked outside, he knew it had to be bad. Anthony Stone stepped foot inside the house and couldn't believe his eyes. He walked over to another officer. "Tell me that's not what I think it is in there!" He growled. "Tell me those are not children's body parts in there!"

"We have to find this guy before he can strike again," the officer said with a serious look on his face. Anthony Stone entered the other room and it took everything in him not to throw up.

"Detective we found this," another officer said handing Anthony Stone an envelope. He looked down and saw that the envelope was address to him. Anthony Stone opened the envelope and began reading.

"Hello Anthony Stone the purpose of this letter is to let you know that the gloves are off and I'm done playing with you. You want to stick your nose in Uncle Sam's business, now you are Uncle Sam's business. You now have a front row view...hope YOU enjoy the show.

Sincerely yours: Uncle Sam."

"I want this entire house dusted for prints!" Anthony Stone ordered. This Uncle Sam character was really starting to piss him off. Anthony Stone knew if he planned on catching the serial killer, then he would have to keep a leveled head and not run off of his emotions. This was turning into an intense chess match. There was something different about this crime scene, all of Uncle Sam previous murder victims had been all females. Anthony Stone found something funny about finding the dead children inside the house, something about this wasn't right and he planned on getting to the bottom of it as soon as possible.

48 HΣURS TO DIE

CHAPTER 18

"Explain"

Reggie and Lisa sat in a booth in the back of a fancy restaurant downtown enjoying a nice dinner. After what happened the other night, neither one of them wanted to address the situation, but unfortunately, it had to be addressed. "What happen the other night?" Reggie asked taking a sip of his wine.

"Sorry, I saw those kids and kind of freaked out," Lisa apologized. "For it to be my first time I wasn't expecting that I thought you were going to kind of like ease me in there."

"I figured we might as well get the hard part out of the way first," Reggie smiled. "Are you sure you want to do this?"

"Yes of course," Lisa answered quickly. The last thing she wanted was for Reggie to think that she couldn't handle the pressure of taking a human life.

Reggie took another sip from his wine. "How many people did you tell about my little secret?"

"I didn't tell anyone," she told him. "What would they think of me if I continued to work at the club knowing what I know?"

"True," Reggie finished off his drink only to refill his wine glass back to the top. "If you're going to work with me then you're going to have to keep your mouth shut and you can't be scared to take a life, this is what I do."

"How can you be around all that blood like that and it not bother you?" Lisa asked.

"It takes time baby."

"Oh, I'm your baby now?" Lisa blushed.

Reggie returned her smile. "Of course you are," he lied just to keep her comfortable. He had to keep her feeling comfortable and wanted so she wouldn't roll over on him. "You think we would be at this nice restaurant if you weren't my baby?" He said laying it on thick.

"I'm just happy that you're not mad at me about what happen the other night," Lisa breathed a sigh of relief.

"I'm not mad but the next time we go out hunting you better be ready," he said with a raised brow.

"I promise you I won't mess up like I did the last time," Lisa promised thankful to be giving another opportunity to prove herself.

Reggie smiled. "You see that lady over there?" Lisa turn and saw women entering the restroom.

"That lady going to the restroom?"

Reggie nodded. "I want you to go and in the bathroom and put a bullet in her head."

Immediately, a look of nervousness came over Lisa's face. "Huh? You want me to kill her now? In the restaurant?" She whispered.

Reggie pulled out a .380 with a silencer attached to the barrel and slid it to, Lisa under the table. "You don't have much time."

Lisa took the gun, stuck it down inside of her pocket book, then stood up and quickly headed towards the restroom.

Reggie sat back with a smirk on his face as he continued to sip from his glass of wine. "This should be good," he said to himself.

***

Lisa entered the bathroom and was happy when she noticed that she and her target were the only ones in the restroom at the time. Lisa quickly pulled the .380 from her pocketbook, afraid that someone was going to bust in while she was committing a murder she moved quick. Lisa walked over towards the stall that her target occupied. She entered the stall next to her target, stood on the toilet seat, looked over to the next stall, and saw the woman letting out some food that must not have upset her stomach. Lisa stuck her arm over in the next stall and said, "Hey!" When the lady looked up, Lisa pulled the trigger dumping three bullets into the lady's face. She quickly climbed off the toilet, stuck the gun back inside of her pocketbook, and exited the restroom like normal. Lisa quickly walked back over to over to her table in the cut with a nervous look on her face. "It's done, now come on we have to go!" She said in a harsh whisper. Reggie smiled as he slowly stood to his feet, dropped a few bills down on the table, grabbed Lisa's hand, and led her out of the restaurant.

When Reggie and Lisa stepped foot inside Lisa's apartment, Reggie roughly grabbed her and slammed her against the wall. Before Lisa could even say a word, Reggie stuck his tongue in her mouth as the two enjoyed a long drawn out sloppy kiss. Lisa taking that woman's life in the restaurant had turned Reggie on. He aggressively ripped Lisa's blouse open and kissed all up and down her neck while removing her bra all at the same time. Once Lisa's bra was off, Reggie popped one of her breast in his mouth like a savage.

"Mmm!" Lisa moaned loudly as she hopped up on, Reggie locking her toned legs around his waist as he carried her into the bedroom and slammed her down on the bed. Reggie lifted Lisa's skirt up and forcefully tore her thong off of her bottom with his bare hands. Before Lisa got a chance to catch her breath, she felt, Reggie's tongue on the magic button in between her legs. "Awww!" She pure with her head back in ecstasy.

Reggie licked, Lisa's warm, wet slice nice and slow like this would be his last time ever tasting a woman again. He worked his tongue like a lizard as felt, Lisa's body squirming under him. Reggie rolled his tongue back and forth on, Lisa's clit until he felt her legs violently clamp around his neck. He found pleasure in her body jerking uncontrollably under his touch. Reggie slid his way in between, Lisa's legs and slid inside her. "Hmmm!" He groaned as the heat and the wetness from Lisa's vagina had him in another world. Reggie pinned, Lisa's back towards her head and did pushups on top of her as his rod dipped in and out of her wetness. Reggie worked his hips like a Latin dancer as he plunged in and out of Lisa.

"Ye... yes...yes...don't stop...just like...that!" Lisa growled all of her class and lady as if ways were gone; Reggie had her in complete freak mode.

Reggie delivered four more quick strokes before he grunted and collapsed on top of, Lisa. "Oh my god," he whispered breathing heavily. Reggie stared up at the ceiling as; Lisa crawled in his arms and laid her head on his chest. The two laid like that in silence until they finally drifted off to sleep.

48 HӠURS TO DIE

CHAPTER 19

"Mind Playing Tricks On Me"

After a long day at work, Anthony Stone was happy to be on his way home. He rode in his car as Drake's new album hummed softly through the speakers. He bobbed his head to the beat as he pulled in front of his apartment building. Anthony Stone stepped out of his car and headed towards his building. As he got closer to the building, he noticed a man standing in front of his building with a hoodie on with his hands in pockets of the hoodie. Something about the man just looked suspicious, besides Anthony Stone knew all the tenants that resided in his building, and the man with the hoodie on didn't look familiar. Anthony Stone walked up to the man in the hoodie. "Can I help you?"

The hooded man looked Anthony Stone up and down. "Nah I'm good,"

"Are you visiting somebody in this building or something?" Anthony Stone pried.

"No, I'm minding my business," the hoodie man said. His tone was hostile as if he was getting ready for a confrontation. "Fuck off!"

"I'm going to need to see some Identification," Anthony Stone said taking a few steps closer to the hooded man invading his personal space.

The hooded man looked at Anthony Stone as if he was insane. "Get out my face!" He barked. "I'm not going to tell you again!" He threatened, his hands now turning into fist.

"I need to see some identification!" Anthony Stone said in a stern tone as he flashed his badge. The hooded man looked down at the badge and took off running. He only made it a few feet away before Anthony Stone roughly tackled the hooded man face first down to the concrete. "Stop resisting!" Anthony Stone struggled to get the man's hands behind his back. Once the hooded man was hand cuffed, Anthony Stone fished through the man's pockets until he heard a woman's voice behind him.

"Anthony, what are you doing?" Amy asked with a nervous and concerned look on her face. She lived in the same building two floors above Anthony Stone.

"Amy stay back!" Anthony Stone said. "This man could be dangerous,"

"He's my boyfriend," Amy called out. "Did he break any laws?"

Anthony Stone pulled the hooded man up to his feet. "Why didn't you just tell me you were waiting for Amy?"

"Because it's none of your damn business who I'm waiting for!" The hooded man barked as Anthony Stone removed the cuffs from his wrist. "I want your name and badge number!" He barked.

"I'm sorry," Anthony Stone apologized. Uncle Sam had his mind playing tricks on him; he was so stuck on catching the serial killer that it messed up his judgment. "Amy I'm sorry about that," he said then disappeared inside his apartment building.

48 HΞURS TO DIE

CHAPTER 20

"Showtime"

The next evening, Lisa sat at the bar alone. For the past hour, she'd been throwing beers back left and right. Her heavy drinking had grabbed the attention of a heavyset man that sat at the end of the bar nursing a drink. His intentions were to hopefully find a chick that had a bit too much to drink, take her home, and take advantage of her. When the right moment presented itself, the big man eased his way down the bar and helped himself to the open seat next to Lisa.

"Hey beautiful," the big man said with a smile. Lisa gave the big man a once over and returned his smile. "Heeeey how are you?" She sang acting more intoxicated than she really was.

"What you doing in a place like this all by yourself?" The big man asked.

"Just needed a quick getaway, you know," Lisa chuckled, playing the role of a drunk woman perfectly. Anyone on the outside looking in would have sworn that the woman at the bar was wasted.

"A getaway from what?" The big man asked. "Listen; if someone is bothering you I can protect you."

Lisa rubbed the big man's arm seductively. "Hey I think I've had one too many, do you mind walking me out to my car?"

"Sure," the big man said happily. This was the opportunity he was waiting for. A chance to get the woman outside and away from all the eyes in the bar. The big man escorted Lisa outside. "Where are you parked?" He asked placing his arm on the small of her back.

"Two blocks down," Lisa slurred as she felt the big man's hand slide down to her butt sneaking some cheap feels. The big man's hand all over her disgusted her, but she continued to play the role. Lisa led the big man down a dark street and headed towards a Honda Accord. "Thank you so much for making sure I made it to my car safe I really appreciate it."

"The pleasure was all mine," the big man said invading, Lisa's personal space. The big man got ready to let his hands explore Lisa when he heard somebody loudly clear their throat behind him. The big man spun around and saw a man in a hoodie with his head down holding an ax in his hands. "What the hell is going on?" The big man asked in a panic tone. He reached down in his pocket and removed his cell phone so he could call the police, but before he could press the first number, Lisa jammed a knife repeatedly down into the side of the big man's neck until he crumbled down to the floor.

Reggie walked up, looked at Lisa, and smiled when her saw her face covered in specs of blood. Without warning, Reggie lifted the ax over his head, and then brought it down with tremendous force repeatedly until there were no more body parts left to cut. Reggie looked up right in time to see Lisa heave and throw up all the food that she had consumed earlier right on the ground. It was at that very moment he knew he was going to have to kill Lisa. Her DNA now laid on the concrete of a murder scene. Just as he predicted, she wasn't built for this type of life. Reggie knew that before sunrise, the cops would be at Lisa's doorstep questioning her. If he had to bet, he was sure that if the right amount of pressure were applied she would give him up without thinking twice. "Come on we have to get out of here!" Reggie said as they both slipped inside the Honda Accord and peeled off.

***

Lisa parked the Honda in her garage, killed the engine, then turned and faced Reggie. "Sorry about what happened back there," she apologized as if that would fix everything. "You not mad at me are you?"

"Of course not," Reggie lied. "As a matter of fact the exact same thing happened to me on my first time," he lied again with a straight face.

"What now?" Lisa asked feeling a little better since Reggie didn't seem to be mad with her.

"First things first, we have to go inside take off our clothes and burn them. Then we have to clean off our weapons and get rid of them."

Lisa entered her house through the garage, with Reggie close on her heels before she even got a chance to sit her keys down on the counter, Reggie swung the ax with all his might, and chopped Lisa's head clean off of her shoulders. It took a couple of seconds for Lisa's body to respond and crumble down to the floor. Reggie looked down at Lisa's decapitated body and shook his head with a disgusted look on his face.

48 HƎURS TO DIE

CHAPTER 21

"What Now?"

Anthony Stone pulled up on the deserted street that was full of cops and flashing lights. When his phone rung in the middle of the night he knew that whatever it was it had to be bad. He walked and immediately spotted a males body part on the ground. "What do we have here?"

"Male, mid-thirties, found chopped up," the officer said, then handed Anthony Stone an envelope. "It's addressed to you."

Anthony Stone took the envelope and opened it, and began to read the letter inside.

"Good evening Detective Stone, if you are reading this then once again that means you have failed to protect the innocent tax payers that pays your salary. Looks like I'm going to have to turn up the heat a little to get you to do your job, if things go according to plan then I'm sure I'll be seeing you face to face soon...

Sincerely yours: Uncle Sam."

Anthony Stone handed the envelope back to the officer. "Any idea where this guy was coming from?"

"Not sure but I saw a bar a few blocks down that would be my best guess," the officer replied. "Also it looks like our killer may have thrown up; we're getting that checked now for DNA."

"I'm going over to the bar to check it out," Anthony Stone said. "Keep me posted on that vomit," he called over his shoulder.

Anthony Stone entered the bar, walked up to the bartender, and flashed his badge. "Detective Stone I'm going to need to have a look at your surveillance tapes."

"I'm sorry but only the owner is authorized to touch the surveillance tapes," the bartender replied.

"Then I suggest you get him on the phone."

***

An hour later Anthony Stone sat in the back office along with the owner of the bar looking over the surveillance tapes. "Pause it right there and zoom in," he said trying to get a good look at the woman's face. "I've seen her somewhere before," he said out loud. Anthony Stone turned to face another detective who was in the room. "Run her image through our data base and let me know what comes up!" He ordered. Stone turned back and faced the bar owner. "Thank you so much for your cooperation,"

Anthony Stone stepped out the bar was immediately met by Captain Fisher. "Hey captain what's up?"

"The chick from the bar her name is Lisa Montgomery. Her record is clean. Just a few parking tickets. Last place of employment was some club called, Club Blaze," Captain Fisher informed him.

As soon as Anthony Stone heard the name Club Blaze, it all came back to him. He remembered the Latin woman who claimed to be the manager of Club Blaze the same club where, Melissa was last seen before her body showed up in the trunk of an abandoned car. "You have an address for me?"

"Already texted it to you," Captain Fisher said with a smirk.

48 HЗURS TO DIE

CHAPTER 22

"Hands Where I Can See Them"

Anthony Stone pulled up in front of Lisa's home just in time to see cops dressed in riot gear, battery ram the front door down and swarm inside the residence. He waited until the place was secure before he entered. Anthony Stone stepped foot inside the house and immediately the smell of a dead body and blood assaulted his nostrils. He walked further inside the house and saw what he suspected to be Lisa's body parts scattered throughout the kitchen and blood everywhere. Anthony Stone felt his phone vibrating on his hip; he looked down at the screen and saw, Captain Fisher's name flashing. "Yeah," he answered.

"Do you have Lisa in custody?" Captain Fisher asked. "Got the results back from the lab and the DNA from the vomit belongs to Lisa."

"By the time we got here she was already dead, chopped up in little pieces," Anthony Stone told him.

"What are you thinking?"

"I think our killer is the owner of Club Blaze," Anthony Stone said. "Some creep named Reggie Braxton, Lisa worked for him. So I'm suspecting he was using her to help him kill his victims, she didn't have the stomach for it and threw up."

"Uncle Sam knew we'd track her down so he killed her before she got the chance to rat him out."

"Exactly," Anthony Stone agreed.

"What do we have on this creep, Reggie?"

"Not much," Anthony Stone said honestly. "If we bring him in now the charges definitely wouldn't stick."

"Go to his house and see what you can find out, you didn't hear that from me," Captain Fisher said, then ended the conversation.

Anthony Stone exited, Lisa's house and headed straight for Reggie's house.

48 HΞURS TO DIE

CHAPTER 23

"Last House On The Left"

Anthony Stone cruised through the gated community at a slow speed not wanting to miss the house he was looking for. From the first time that he laid eyes on Reggie, he got a bad feeling about the man. He still wasn't a hundred percent sure if Reggie was his man, but his gut was telling him something different. Anthony Stone pulled up into the circular driveway. The house was beautiful and big enough to house three or maybe four families. Anthony Stone walked up to the front door and rang the doorbell.

***

Reggie stood in the bathroom of his basement washing Lisa's blood from his hands. He felt bad about killing Lisa but he had to do what he had to do. He still wasn't sure if Lisa had told anyone about his little secret only time would tell. As Reggie stood in the basement, he wondered if the police had made it to Lisa's house yet. He knew that maybe the police would be able to link Lisa to him, now he just had to hope and pray that she hadn't told anyone about his dark side. Reggie dried his hands when he noticed detective Anthony Stone through his surveillance camera at his front door. Reggie took his sweet time walking upstairs, and then finally made his way to the front door. He opened the door a crack and stuck his head out. "Good evening detective may I help you?"

"Yes I have a few questions I want to ask you, may I come inside?"

"I'm sorry detective do you have a warrant?" Reggie asked with a raised brow

"No, but I just wanted to ask you a few...."

"I'm sorry detective," Reggie said cutting, Anthony Stone off. "I'm a very busy man and if you don't have a warrant or if I'm not under arrest I'm going to have to ask you to leave," he said with a phony smile on his face. "Thanks for dropping by," he said, then slammed the door in the detective's face.

Reggie walked over and flopped down on his couch. He didn't like how close Anthony Stone was coming to putting the case together. Things were getting too close for his liking. He had to think of a way to get the detective off of his back for good. Reggie sat thinking until he finally came up with a genius idea on how to get rid of detective Stone once and for all.

48 HOURS TO DIE

CHAPTER 24

"From Bad To Worst"

Anthony Stone sat at his desk on his computer trying to find as much information on Reggie as possible. He didn't know what it was about the man, but something about him just rubbed him the wrong way. Anthony Stone could tell that it was something going on that Reggie wasn't telling him. Now he had to figure out and find a way to get a warrant to search Reggie's home and his office at the club.

It had been going on two weeks since the last time Anthony Stone had heard from Uncle Sam and honestly, he was happy to not hear from the serial killer, no news was always good news in his book. Anthony Stone knew that in order to catch a serial killer he would have to begin to think like one. He would have to be one step ahead if he planned on ever capturing Uncle Sam. Anthony Stone sat behind his desk when he heard his cell phone ringing. He glanced down at the screen and saw, Tasha's name flashing across the screen. "Hey baby," he answered.

"Hey love of my life," Tasha sang in an upbeat tone. "What are you doing right now?"

"At my desk still working on this case, what you up too?" Anthony Stone yawned.

"Nothing just working on your surprise,"

"What surprise?" Anthony Stone asked.

"Well I guess you'll have to come home and find out," Anthony Stone could picture, Tasha's bright smile through the phone.

"I'll swing by your mother's house in about an hour."

"I'm not at my mother's house."

"Where are you?" Anthony Stone asked his tone dead serious now.

"At your apartment," Tasha sang happily. "I know you said not to come here, but I wanted to surprise you," she said. "That Uncle Sam guy is just trying to get into your head, plus I'm tired of sleeping by myself every night," she whined.

"Tasha listen to me, get your stuff, and get out of that apartment right now!" Anthony Stone said as he heard his phone beep notifying him that someone was on his other line. "Hold on real quick baby," he said and clicked over. "Detective Stone here," he answered.

"Hello detective," the voice on the other line said in a robotic tone. "Whatever Tasha's cooking it sure smells good what the special occasion is?" He said followed by a sickening laugh. Anthony Stone quickly clicked over to the other line. "Tasha! Get out of that apartment right now!"

"Baby calm down what's wrong?"

"Uncle Sam is somewhere in the building get out of there right now! I'm on my way!" Anthony Stone said ending the call. He hung up yelled over his shoulder. "He's at my house!" And flew out the door. He was determined to not let Uncle Sam kill Tasha. "Not today!" He growled as he got behind the wheel of his Charger and pulled out into traffic like a mad man.

48 HOURS TO DIE

CHAPTER 25

"Who's There?"

Tasha hung the phone up, threw on a pair of leggings and a tank top, and exited the apartment. She stepped out into the hallway taking hurried steps. She hit the call button for the elevator repeatedly. As Tasha stood waiting for the elevator, she heard the staircase door squeak open; she looked down the hall and spotted a man in a black hoodie headed in her direction power walking towards her with something in his hand.

"Oh shit!" Tasha yelled as she took off in a sprint down the hall. She looked over her shoulder and saw the hooded man chasing behind her with a black object in his hand that looked like a gun. Tasha quickly ran into the opposite staircase and began taking hurried steps down the stairs just as bullets whizzed by her head and echoed loudly off the staircase walls.

***

Reggie took off after Tasha and chased her into the staircase where he aimed his gun above her head and fired three thunderous shots that slammed into the wall. The shots weren't meant to kill or harm Tasha he just wanted to scare her. Reggie chased Tasha down the stairs until he got close enough and dived from the top of the steps and landed on Tasha's back tackling her down the remaining steps. The two tumbled down to the next landing. Reggie quickly made in to his feet, pulled out a needle, and jammed into Tasha's thigh, he then lifted her up off the floor and tossed her over his shoulder like a sack of potatoes and carried her down to the lobby. Several people looked on with concern as the hooded man carried a woman through the lobby draped over his shoulder.

"Somebody call 911!" A woman yelled.

"Hey where are you taking that woman?" A man in glasses called out. Reggie walked through the lobby with head down so no one could get a good look at his face as he ignored all the people and exited the lobby. Reggie stepped out of the building where his getaway car awaited him. He popped the trunk and roughly tossed Tasha's body down into the trunk not caring where it landed. Reggie slammed the trunk just as Anthony Stone pulled up to a screeching halt on the opposite side of the street.

48 HOURS TO DIE

CHAPTER 26

"Don't Do It"

Anthony Stone pulled up in front of his building just in time to see a hooded man tossing a female in the back of his trunk. He couldn't tell for sure if the female being tossed in the back of, the trunk was Tasha, but his gut was telling him that it was definitely, Tasha. "Freeze!" Anthony Stone yelled with his 9mm aimed at the hooded man.

Reggie spun and opened fire on the detective forcing him to take cover behind a work van. Reggie then quickly hopped behind the wheel of his vehicle and pulled recklessly out into the street.

Once the gunfire stopped, Anthony Stone sprang from behind the van and opened fire on the hooded man's vehicle, shattering the entire back window. Anthony Stone ran towards the car trying to get a better shot when the driver pulled out into the street like a mad man. Without thinking twice, Anthony Stone took off in a sprint and jumped up on top of a parked car. He ran down the line of parked cars, then leaped through the air and violently landed on the roof of the hooded man's car losing control of his gun in the landing process. Anthony Stone held on to the edges of the roof of the car as the driver merged onto the highway and gunned the engine.

Reggie swerved from lane to lane-going 90 mph, purposely trying to sling Anthony Stone from the roof of his car. He cut the steering wheel hard to the right jumping two lanes over, and then cut the steering wheel back over to the left. Reggie went to jump over to the next lane when Anthony Stone's hand came crashing through the window and wrapped around his throat. Reggie lost control of the vehicle for second as he tried to pry Anthony Stone's hand from around his throat with one hand and held a firm grip on the steering wheel with his other hand. The more, Reggie struggled with Anthony Stone, the stronger the grip around his throat seem to become. Having no other choice, Reggie grabbed the gun that rested on his lap and fired three shots up into the roof of the car.

"Arggghhh!" Anthony Stone growled as one of the hooded man's bullets exploded in the chest area of his Kevlar vest forcing him to release his grip on the roof of the car with his left hand. The hooded man then suddenly stomped down hard on the brakes; the momentum forcing caused Anthony Stone to go flying off the roof of the car.

His body violently bounced off the concrete and rolled for about ten seconds before coming to a complete stop. Anthony Stone lifted his head up and saw the headlights of the hooded man's car coming straight at him full speed.

48 HEURS TO DIE

CHAPTER 27

"What Now?"

nthony Stone rolled out of the way just as the car zoomed pass. His heart was beating at an all-time high. It didn't bother him that he had almost lost his life, what really bothered him was the fact that he wasn't able to save Tasha's life. Anthony Stone watched with tears in his eyes as the tail lights of the car disappeared into the night.

It was at the very moment that he knew the chances of him seeing Tasha alive again were slim.

While the EMT workers worked on Anthony Stone's shoulder, his mind was on Tasha. Inside he felt bad as if it was his fault that, Tasha was probably somewhere in some dark basement begging for her life. Captain Fisher walked up with a sad look on his face. "Don't worry, Stone we're going to catch this sicko if it's the last thing that we do!"

Anthony Stone wiped his eyes. He loved Captain Fisher like an uncle but right now, his words were going in one ear and out the other. All he could think about was Tasha. He could only imagine what she was thinking and going through right now. Because of him and his job, the love of his life was now in the trunk of a car probably on her way to get chopped up into little pieces.

"Pull yourself together," Captain Fisher said. "We're going to catch this scumbag if it's the last thing we do."

Anthony Stone stood to his feet and walked over towards, Captain Fisher's car. "I need a ride home," he said with his head hung low in a defeated tone. Captain Fisher could tell that Detective Stone was hurting on the inside, usually he was good at hiding it, but this time he couldn't hide it even if he wanted to.

"Come on partner lets go have a drink I'm buying," Captain Fisher said as him and Anthony Stone got in his car. For the entire car ride Anthony Stone was silent, he sat leaned back in his seat with his eyes closed. A million different things were running through his mind at the moment, and he had no clue where to start.

"Take me to Tasha's mother's house,"

"Huh?"

"Ms. Brown, take me to Ms. Brown's house I need to make sure that she's still alive!" Anthony Stone suddenly remembered.

"Who?" Captain Fisher said with a confused look on his face.

"Tasha's mother," Anthony Stone explained. He gave, Captain Fisher the address and prayed that nothing had happened to Ms. Brown.

Twenty minutes later, Captain Fisher came to a screeching stop in front of Ms. Brown's house. Anthony Stone stepped out of the passenger seat with his back up gun in his hand. He took cautious steps over towards the patrol car that sat parked in front of the house, while Captain Fisher headed for the front of the house. When Anthony Stone got close to the patrol car, he noticed that the front windshield was shattered and two small bullet holes rested in the center. Anthony Stone made it to the driver's window and saw the officer that was supposed to be watching over and protecting the property slumped with his head leaning over to the side, his face was covered in a mask of blood.

"Damn!" Anthony Stone yelled in frustration. If the officer was dead, he could only imagine what Uncle Sam had done to, Ms. Brown. He walked over towards the front door when he saw Captain Fisher coming out of the house.

"Is she...?"

"There's nobody in the house," Captain Fisher told him. "I searched the entire house from top to bottom."

"We have an officer down over in the patrol car," Anthony Stone explained.

"What do you think this scumbag is up too?" Captain Fisher asked.

Anthony Stone shook his head sadly. "I have no idea, but whatever it is it can't be good."

48 HZURS TO DIE

CHAPTER 28

"Where Am I?"

Tasha laid balled up in the back of the dark trunk with a scared expression on her face. She had no clue where this crazy hooded man was taking her. Tasha held on to the sides of the trunk as she felt the road go from smooth to rough and bumpy. Minutes later, she felt the vehicle slow down, and then stop. Immediately, she began reaching around for something she could use as a weapon. She sucked her teeth when she came up empty. Seconds later, the trunk swung open, Uncle Sam reached down and roughly snatched Tasha out of the trunk by her hair. Tasha screamed as the hooded man dragged her across the concrete in what looked to be some kind of abandoned warehouse. Tasha reached up and tried to drag her nails down the hooded man's face, but instead she caught his neck.

"Bitch!" Uncle Sam growled as he turned and slapped Tasha across the face so hard that her chin touched her shoulder. "I see I'm going to have to teach you some manners!" He growled as he pulled out a roll of duct tape and taped Tasha's hands behind her back. Uncle Sam dragged Tasha by the ankles until they reached the middle of the warehouse where he picked her up and forcefully slammed her down into a wooden chair where he placed a piece of duct tape around Tasha's mouth. He then bound her ankles and her waist to the chair.

Tasha looked over to her right and saw her mother bounded down to the chair next to her. From the blood that covered Ms. Brown's face, Tasha could tell that the hooded man had done a number on her. Not being able to speak, the mother and daughter had to speak through their eyes. The first thing Tasha did was try to look around to see if she noticed something familiar so she could try and tell where she was, but it was no use, the warehouse doors were close and the windows were too high for her to see out of. Tasha looked over and could see the scared and frightened look on her mother's face, she wanted to tell her mother that everything was going to be alright, but when she saw the hooded man setting up a tripod with a camera on top she knew things were about to go from bad to worst.

48 HEURS TO DIE

CHAPTER 29

"Nightmare"

For the past three days, Anthony Stone stayed inside his apartment. He couldn't function or think straight all he could think about was, Tasha and her mother being tortured and begging for their lives. "It's all my fault," Anthony Stone cried, once again his work had somehow spilled over into his personal life. He poured himself a glass of vodka and took a deep sip, then crumbled his face up as it went down. Anthony Stone sat on the sofa drinking his life away when he heard a light knock at his front door. He hopped up off the sofa, grabbed his 9mm, and quickly made his way over toward the front door. Anthony Stone snatched the door open and found a UPS worker standing on the other side. "Can I help you?"

"Yes I have a package for a Mr. Anthony Stone," The deliveryman said holding out a clipboard towards Anthony Stone. Anthony Stone signed for the package then closed the door, making his way back over to the couch. Before opening, the package he placed his ear to the side first to make sure whatever was inside wasn't ticking. Once he was sure that it wasn't a bomb Anthony Stone slowly opened the packed and saw that it was a DVD with the words "read me" taped on to the case. Without hesitation, Anthony Stone popped the DVD into the DVD player and pressed play. Seconds later and mask man appeared on the screen and began to speak with a robotic, electronic tone.

"If you're seeing this video then that means things have gotten way out of hand and therefore one of us has to go," The mask man said. The camera then suddenly switched over towards, Tasha and her mother sitting tied down in separate chairs. Anthony Stone could immediately see the fear on both of their faces. He watched as the mask man ordered Ms. Brown to keep still as he reappeared in the video holding an ax in his hand. The mask man turned and looked into the camera, smiled; he then turned raised the ax and chopped Ms. Brown's foot off.

Anthony Stone was forced to watch in horror as blood sprayed all over the floor as Ms. Brown released a muffled scream, the look on her face said that she was in tremendous pain. The more Anthony Stone watched the angrier he became. It was killing him to have to watch his woman's mother in so much pain.

Seconds later, the mask man got back in front of the camera. "Anthony Stone you have forty eight hours to either kill yourself or watch your family die. The choice is yours!" And just like that, the video ended.

Anthony Stone watched the video over and over. He knew that even if he was to take his own life that there was still a chance that Uncle Sam could still kill Tasha and her mother anyway. Anthony Stone tossed his glass against the wall out of frustration. "Forty eight hours to die," he murmured looking down at the 9mm in his hand. Anthony Stone hopped up and quickly got dress, he didn't have forty-eight hours to die, but instead forty-eight hours to find Uncle Sam.

48 HZURS TO DIE

CHAPTER 30

"I See You"

That same night, Anthony Stone sat camped out five houses down from, Reggie's huge estate. He wasn't positive on who Uncle Sam was for sure, but all signs pointed to Reggie. It was just something about him that just rubbed Anthony Stone the wrong way. After two hours of staking out, he noticed Reggie's Bentley pull into his circular driveway. Anthony Stone sat behind the wheel of his car looking through a pair of high-powered binoculars.

He watched as Reggie exited the Bentley wearing black sweat pants and a hooded sweatshirt. He then walked back towards the trunk, reached in and removed a duffle bag, then disappeared through the front door of his house.

Anthony Stone immediately got a bad vibe. Everything about Reggie looked suspicious as if he was hiding something. First things first Anthony Stone wanted to know what, Reggie carried inside that duffle bag that he carried inside the house.

After sitting for about twenty minutes, Anthony Stone watched as Reggie exited the house in an expensive suit walking fast as if he was in a rush. He watched as Reggie climbed inside his luxury car and pulled off. Anthony Stone ducked down in his seat as the Bentley zoomed past him in a hurry. Anthony Stone sat in his car for ten minutes before he exited his car, slipped a hood over his head, and slowly walked towards Reggie's house. He knew what he was about to do was wrong and against the law, but at the moment he had to take the law in his own hands. Anthony Stone needed answers and those answers were on the other said of those mansion doors. He jogged in a low crouch until he reached a door at the back of the house. Anthony Stone pulled out a drill gun and quickly began to remove the screws from the lock on the door. Seven minutes later, Anthony Stone entered the house with his 9mm in one hand and his Maglite in the other. He slowly eased his way throughout the house looking for anything that could connect Reggie to the murders. Anthony Stone walked slowly throughout the house and stopped when he saw a door that looked to be out of place. He walked over, snatched the door open, and found steps that led down to the basement. Anthony Stone slowly made his way down the stairs, when his feet touched the bottom landing, he couldn't believe his eyes. All throughout the basement were killing tools. A torture bed rested in the center of the basement. Anthony Stone saw everything from knives, guns, axes, and any other killing object one could think of. The more Anthony Stone looked around the more he worried about Tasha and Ms. Brown, now knowing that Reggie was indeed Uncle Sam. Anthony Stone exited the basement and headed upstairs to the master bedroom to see what else he could find. The light from his Maglite guided Anthony Stone throughout the lavish property. Anthony Stone reached the bedroom and began searching for more evidence he reached, Reggie's dresser and shone his light on a pile of envelopes, the same type of envelopes that, Uncle Sam left at all of his crime scenes next to the envelopes were several pictures in nice frames that lined up nice and neat next to one another. Immediately, Anthony Stone recognized the woman's face that was in most of the pictures. There were pictures of a woman that he had failed to save during a hostage situation a few years ago. Now putting the pieces together, Anthony Stone realized that the woman was none other than, Reggie's wife. "So that's why he's doing all of this?" He whispered to himself. Anthony Stone made his way over towards, Reggie's closet and stopped in mid-stride when he saw the duffle bag sitting on the floor. He looked down inside the bag and the first thing he saw was a roll of duct tape with hairs sticking from it, Anthony Stone stuffed the roll of tape down into his pocket. Just as he was about to continue to search the duffle bag, he heard the front door slam shut informing him that he was no longer alone in the house.

48 HOURS TO DIE

CHAPTER 30

"Who's In My House?"

Reggie made it four blocks away before he realized that he had left his phone charger on the counter. Without thinking twice, he made a U-turn and headed back to the house. Reggie smiled at the thought of having the upper hand on Detective Stone; he could only imagine what was going on in the detective's mind at this very moment. Reggie felt no remorse for what he was doing, he had to sit back and watch his wife die, and now it was Anthony

Stone's turn to suffer the same way he did. Reggie pulled into his driveway, kept the engine running, and ran inside the house. Reggie stepped foot inside his home, walked over to the counter and grabbed his charger. He turned to make his exit but stopped when he heard what sounded like footsteps coming from upstairs. Reggie stood still for a second and listened carefully. A few seconds passed with complete silence. Just as Reggie was about to head towards the door, he heard the noise again. He quickly removed the .45 from the small of his back and headed upstairs to investigate.

Reggie made it to the top of the steps and the first place he searched was the first bathroom. He slowly eased opened the door trying to be as quiet as possible. He stepped further into the bathroom and snatched the shower curtain back ready to shoot. He breathed a sigh of relief when he saw that the tub was empty. Reggie exited the bathroom and continued down the long hallway until he reached one of the many guest rooms. He slowly eased the door open and searched the entire room. Empty.

Reggie stepped out the guest room and headed straight for the master bedroom. He eased the room door open and instantly something didn't feel right. He inched his way inside the room and the first thing he did was check under the bed. Empty. Reggie then slowly made his way over to the closet, when the sound of a cell phone ringing could be heard coming from inside the closet. Without warning, he fired five shots into the closet door. Reggie waited a few seconds before he slowly raised his hand and snatched the closet door open.

48 HEURS TO DIE

CHAPTER 31

"I Know It's You"

Anthony Stone hid in the closet trying to be as quiet as he possibly could. He reached around the closet and found an all-black ski mask more evidence that just confirmed that Reggie was indeed Uncle Sam. He listened carefully as he heard someone enter the bedroom. Anthony Stone slowly slid the ski mask down over his face, he knew that if he was to get caught breaking into Reggie's home without a warrant that he would lose his job and possibly face jail time, not to mention that Reggie would more than likely sue the pants off of his department. Anthony Stone stood as quiet as he possibly could when suddenly his cell phone began to ring. He quickly hit the button to silence his phone but it was too late. Seconds later, several gunshots ripped through the closet door. Anthony Stone pressed his back up against the wall and waited. When the closet door opened, he sprung from the closet and charged Reggie full speed. Anthony Stone hit Reggie hard as the two want crashing on the bed. Anthony Stone held the wrist that Reggie held the gun in as Reggie sent several shots up into the ceiling and walls until the gun was empty. Reggie kicked the masked man off of him and made it to his feet first. Before the mask man had a chance to do anything, Reggie was all over him. He threw a four-punch combination that landed on the masked man's face. Anthony Stone took the punches well. He weaved Reggie's next punch and landed two punches of his own. He then grabbed Reggie's head and violently slammed it into the wall. Anthony Stone landed a vicious knee to Reggie's face that he partially blocked. Reggie threw a strong right cross that would have broken the masked man's face, but Anthony Stone dodged the punch just in time to see, Reggie's fist go through the wall leaving a huge hole. Anthony Stone took a step back and landed a sidekick that landed in the pit of Reggie's stomach and sent him crashing out into the hallway.

Out in the hallway, Reggie bounced on his toes as if he was a professional boxer with a grin on his face. He held his guards high as he moved in on the masked man, throwing the type of blows that would knock most men out. Anthony Stone blocked most of the punches but a few still managed to slip through his guard. Reggie kicked the mask man on the side of his leg, and then without letting his leg hit the floor, he used the same the leg to fire another kick toward the mask man's head.

The kick to the leg stunned Anthony Stone and he was able to get his arm up just in time to block the kick to the head. He could tell that the rich club owner had taken a few martial arts classes in his day which was fine because Anthony Stone was no stranger when it came to martial arts he too had taken his fair share of classes over the years. Anthony Stone ran and landed a flying elbow that connected in the center of Reggie's forehead. He then finished him off with a roundhouse kick that landed in Reggie's chest and sent him tumbling backwards down the stairs. Anthony Stone stood at the top of the stairs and watched Reggie violently roll down the stairs until he reached the bottom.

Anthony Stone slowly made his way down the stairs as he watched Reggie slowly crawl back up to his feet. He could have easily escaped throughout the back door but he wanted to inflict more pain on the serial killer. He knew what he was doing was wrong and against the law but he couldn't just sit back and continue to let this sicko go around and kill innocent people. Anthony Stone roughly snatched, Reggie up to his feet by the collar of his shirt and backslapped him as if he was a simple woman. He then grabbed Reggie and tossed him into his huge bookshelf that rested against the wall. Anthony Stone kneeled down and punched Reggie dead in his face. He smiled as he watched Reggie spit out a tooth. Anthony Stone was about to try and kick Reggie's head through the wall when he heard a loud banging on the front door.

"POLICE OPEN UP!" the voice on the other side of the door yelled. The gun shots along with all the noise the two men had made during their fight had caused one of the neighbors to call the cops. Anthony Stone readied to creep out the back door, when Reggie quickly hopped to his feet and charged him, and hit him hard, lifting Anthony Stone off of his feet. The two went violently crashing down onto the kitchen table. Anthony Stone kicked Reggie off of him and quickly made it up to his feet just as the police had kicked the front door open.

"Shit!" He cursed as he took off in a sprint down the hall as the two police officers opened fire on him. Anthony Stone dashed out the back door out into the darkness as two bullets exploded through the door inches away from his head. Outside, Anthony ran through the darkness, he looked over his shoulder and noticed one of the officers in pursuit. He quickly ran and hid behind a parked car and removed the ski mask from his face and tossed it under the car. He then stood up and walked back towards the house with his badge in one hand and his gun in the other.

"Drop your weapon!" The officer yelled when he spotted the man coming towards him with a gun in his hand.

"I'm a cop here's my badge," Anthony Stone said as he held out his badge and slowly placed his 9mm on the ground. The officer moved in closer then lowered his weapon.

"Sorry Detective Stone I didn't know that was you," he said recognizing the detective from being all over the news.

"It's okay," Anthony Stone brushed it off. "I just got the call about a noise complaint."

"Yeah from the looks of it, it looks like a break in, I just chased the burglar around here somewhere, but he must have escaped," the officer said proudly.

Anthony Stone and the officer stepped back inside the house and he saw another officer questioning, Reggie. "I'll take it from here," Anthony Stone cut in.

"Good seeing you again, Reggie," he began. "What happen here?"

"Someone broke into my home and attacked me," Reggie said.

"Maybe you should take some self-defense classes," Anthony Stone said not hiding the fact that he didn't like, Reggie. "Is anything missing from your home?"

"I don't know I didn't have a chance to check yet detective," Reggie stood getting up in detective Stone's face. "What happen to your lip," he nodded at Anthony Stone's busted lip.

"Oh this," Anthony Stone smiled. "I had to put hands on some wanna-be tough guy for messing with my family," he said letting, Reggie know that it was indeed him who had beat him up and broken into his home."

Reggie smirked. "I'm sorry to hear about what happened to your girlfriend, I saw on the news that she had been kidnapped. I hope you find her before something bad happens to her."

"If anything happens to my girlfriend and I mean anything, I will personally make sure that Uncle Sam or whoever is responsible for her abduction gets his or her head blown off."

Reggie smiled. "Well detective like they say when playing chess, you better make your next move your best move."

"I will," Anthony Stone, turned and made his exit. When he made it back to his vehicle, the first thing he did was call Captain Fisher.

"Stone what could you possibly want at this time of night?" Fisher growled into the phone.

"Reggie is Uncle Sam!"

"How do you know?"

"Because I broke into his house and found a torture chamber in his basement, along with the same exact envelopes that he leaves at all of his crime scenes," Anthony Stone explained.

"Are you crazy?" Fisher barked. "Don't you know that if you would have gotten caught they would have thrown you in jail?"

"I know captain, but I had to follow my gut," Anthony Stone said. "Is there any way we can get a warrant drawn up?"

"We need evidence, we can't just charge in a courtroom and get a judge to sign off on a warrant based off of a gut feeling," Fisher explained. "Find some evidence and I'll see what I can do about the warrant on my end."

"Deal," Anthony Stone ended the call. He knew that his time was running out and he would have to stop Uncle Sam from killing Tasha and her mother before it was too late. Anthony Stone sat in his car when he remembered he had taken the roll of duct tape from Reggie's duffle bag. He removed the roll of tape from his pocket and saw the hairs stuck to the end of the tape. He smiled as he headed straight to the lab to find out whom those hairs belonged to.

48 HOURS TO DIE

CHAPTER 32

"Figure It Out"

"**A**rgh!" Tasha growled as her chair landed sideways on the cement floor. She had been rocking the chair back and forth until it finally tipped over. Over a few feet away on the floor sat a sharp piece of metal that Tasha had been eying for the last few hours. She slid on her stomach like a snail until she had finally reached the broken piece of metal. Tasha grabbed the piece of metal and began trying to cut through the tape that bonded her wrist together. After about fifteen minutes of sawing through the duct tape, Tasha's wrist were finally free. The first thing she did was remove the tape from her mouth, then cut through the tape on her ankles. She quickly ran over and removed the tape from her mother's mouth and wrist. "Come on momma I have to get you out of here!"

"No I can't make it," Ms. Brown said wincing down at her sawed off ankle. "You go get help I'll be here,"

"I'm not leaving you here!"

"All I'm going to do is slow you down," Ms. Brown explained. "I'm a big girl I'll be okay," she said with a smile. "Go get us some help."

Tasha nodded, then turned and exited the warehouse.

48 HƐURS TO DIE

CHAPTER 33

"DNA"

Anthony Stone stood in the lab patiently waiting for the results from the few strands of hair to come back. He wanted to rip Reggie's head off and he knew the only way he'd be able to do that was if the results from the hair came back belonging to one of Uncle Sam's many murder victims. After a forty-minute wait, a man wearing an all-white gown handed Anthony Stone a folder. He opened the folder and saw the strands of hair belong to none other than Tasha. "Thanks doc!" Anthony Stone said as he jetted out of the building. Once in his car the first thing he did was call Captain Fisher.

"You better have some good news for me," Fisher answered.

"The hair from the duct tape belongs to Tasha!" Anthony Stone announced. "That should be enough evidence to get a warrant drawn up,"

"You're forgetting that we have to explain where we found this roll of duct tape," Captain Fisher reminded him.

"I'll say I found it my apartment building the other night when, Tasha was abducted," Anthony Stone said. "I'll tell them whatever I have to but I need you to get that warrant drawn up for me please," he knew this was his best chance at finding, Tasha and her mother alive. "Please captain we don't have much time."

"I'll see what I can do!" Captain Fisher ended the call.

48 HEURS TO DIE

CHAPTER 34

"Staying Alive"

Tasha ran blindly through the streets barefoot, she tried to flag down cars and get them to stop but it was no use, not many people were willing to stop for a crazy woman running the streets barefoot. Finally, Tasha spotted a gas station a few blocks away. She ran full speed until she finally arrived. She spilled inside the gas station like a mad woman. "I need to use your phone it's an emergency!" She yelled out of breath.

The young man behind the counter reluctantly handed the barefoot woman his cell phone. Tasha grabbed the phone and the first thing she did was call Anthony Stone.

***

After pulling several strings and calling in for favors, Captain Fisher was finally able to get a warrant to search Reggie's home, and club. Anthony Stone stood outside as he watched two officers battery ram the front door. Instantly several cops dressed in riot gear stormed the fancy property. At the moment, all Anthony Stone could do was pray that Reggie was home. He and Captain Fisher entered the home and all they could hear throughout the house were the words, "Clear."

After searching the entire property, there were no signs of Reggie. "Search the place and see if you can find anything that may help us locate where he's keeping Tasha and her mother," Anthony Stone ordered. He looked down at his watch and saw that he only had two hours remaining on the deadline that Uncle Sam had given him. "He's going to kill them," Anthony Stone said in a light whisper.

"Don't talk like that!" Captain Fisher scolded. "We've come too far to give up now! We're going to find your family!"

Anthony Stone nodded when he felt his phone vibrating on his hip; he looked down and saw a number that he didn't recognize. "Detective Stone," he answered.

"Baby it's me."

"Tasha! Where are you?"

"I'm at a gas station right now," she said in a fast pitch tone. "Me and my mother were tied up at some warehouse a few blocks away from this gas station."

"What's the address to the gas station?"

Tasha held the phone out to the man behind the counter. "Give him the address please."

While the clerk gave Anthony Stone the address, Tasha never noticed Reggie in the back of the gas station picking up a few snacks. He quietly crept up on Tasha from behind and smashed a bottle of orange juice over her head. The blow dazed and buckled Tasha's knees, but somehow she managed to keep her footing. Reggie roughly escorted Tasha out of the gas station and tossed her in the trunk of his car; before Reggie could slam the trunk shut, the clerk from the gas station tackled him down to the ground as if he was a linebacker. That distraction was just what Tasha needed. She quickly crawled out of the trunk and took off running down the street in the opposite direction of the warehouse, flailing her arm like a mad woman trying to get the attention of anyone who could help her.

Reggie made it to his feet, pulled his .45 from his waist, and put two bullets in the clerk's chest before hopping in his car and going after Tasha.

48 HOURS TO DIE

CHAPTER 35

"Run"

Tasha ran down the street barefoot looking for anyone that could help her. She heard the gunshots and knew that more than likely; Reggie would soon be back on her trail. Tasha ran until she came across a hotel. She ran inside the hotel like a mad woman. "Call 911!" She yelled. "He's trying to kill me!" She ran towards the hotel security, but instead of the hotel security helping her as she expected, they tackled Tasha down to the floor and restrained her.

Reggie calmly walked inside the hotel and shot two of the front desk clerks in cold blood, he then turned his gun on the security. He watched as Tasha tried to crawl away. "You ruined everything," he growled as he snatched Tasha up to her feet by her hair. "Why couldn't you just stay at the warehouse and wait for me?"

Tasha remained silent as she looked over Reggie's shoulder and noticed Anthony Stone enter the hotel.

"Put the gun down!" Anthony Stone yelled with his gun trained, on Reggie. Reggie quickly positioned, Tasha in front of him and place his gun to the side of her temple.

"Take another step and I'll blow her head off!" Reggie threatened.

"This has nothing to do with her this is between me and you!" Anthony Stone said. "I'm sorry about what happened to your wife if I could have saved her I promise you I would have."

"No you need to feel my pain!" Reggie growled.

"You doing this is not going to bring back your wife," Anthony Stone pointed out. By now the hotel was filled with police with their weapons trained on, Reggie. "There's no way out of here, why don't you let her go?"

Reggie looked down at his watch and shook his head. "Looks like you're out of time detective. Either you take your life or I'm going to hers you decide."

"Listen you don't have to do this," Anthony Stone tried to reason with the serial killer.

"You got twenty seconds," Reggie said with a no nonsense look on his face.

Anthony Stone placed his gun down on the floor, then turned and yelled to all the cops in the hotel, "Hold your fire!" He then turned his attention back to, Reggie. "Let her go and take me instead,"

"Ten...nine...eight,"

"I owe you a rematch from the other night," Anthony Stone threw it out there hoping that, Reggie would grab the bait. "Let's do this man-to-man."

Reggie paused for a second taking the offer into consideration. "You pigs are a bunch of cowards, if I let her go the rest of these pigs will shoot me down just like that," he snapped his fingers.

"You have my word as a man that nobody will shoot you," Anthony Stone turned and looked back at all the officers that stood spread out in the lobby of the hotel. "Nobody shoot that's a direct order, hold your fire!" He yelled.

Reggie smiled as he roughly shoved, Tasha down to the floor as if she was a piece of trash. "Let's do this," he growled as he began making his way towards Detective Stone. He knew that after the fight was over that he would more than likely be shot down like a dog, but at least he would be able to get some pay back on the guy that he felt was responsible for taking his wife's life.

Anthony Stone put his guard up as Reggie rushed him throwing vicious blows with bad intentions. Anthony Stone blocked the first few blows, but the third one managed to slip through his guards. The punch landed square on Anthony Stone's chin causing his legs to wobble out of reflex he reached out and tried to grab, Reggie, but Reggie was too slick. He easily stepped over to the side and landed three vicious upper cuts that jerked the detective's head back. Before Reggie got a chance to land another punch, Anthony Stone scooped his legs from up under him and dumped Reggie on his head. All the police officers in the lobby rooted and cheered loudly for Anthony Stone. Anthony Stone landed two kicks to Reggie's ribs before he finally made it back to his feet. Reggie slipped a jab, grabbed Anthony Stone, and took him for a ride; he belly to belly slammed the detective as if he was a rag doll.

Anthony Stone quickly scrambled back up to his feet and threw, Reggie in a headlock where he delivered several hard blows to the top of his head. Anthony Stone then ran and rammed, Reggie's head into the wall.

Boom!

Reggie lifted Anthony Stone over his head and violently dumped him on his head. Reggie went to stomp, Anthony Stone's head into the floor when his legs were swept from under him. Anthony Stone quickly climbed on top of Reggie and rained blow after blow down on his exposed face until finally Reggie stopped moving. Anthony Stone held his bloody bawled up fist in the air and held it there. Instead of hitting Reggie again, he turned him over on his chest and hand cuffed him. Anthony Stone then walked over and scooped Tasha up in his arms as he hugged her as if he was trying to squeeze the life out of her. "I love you," he said as tears rolled down his face.

"I love you too," Tasha smiled. "Is it finally over?"

"It's finally over," Anthony Stone smiled. He could only imagine how much of a living hell Tasha's life had been for the past couple of days. Now she could finally go home and relax. Anthony Stone watched as Reggie head-butted an officer escaping from his grip. Anthony Stone shook his head sadly when he saw Reggie running towards him and Tasha full speed. Like an old school cowboy, Anthony Stone pulled his gun from his holster and dropped Uncle Sam with five shots to the chest. It was now finally over.

Anthony Stone holster his weapon and was about to leave when he saw Captain Fisher enter the hotel. He walked straight up to Anthony Stone and extended his hand.

"Great work detective," he smiled. "I'm glad this is finally over and your family is safe."

"Me too," Anthony Stone smiled as him and Tasha exited the hotel holding hands.

"I think we need a vacation," Tasha said out loud.

"Yeah you going to definitely need a vacation after I get you home," Anthony Stone said with a devilish smile on his face.

"THE END"

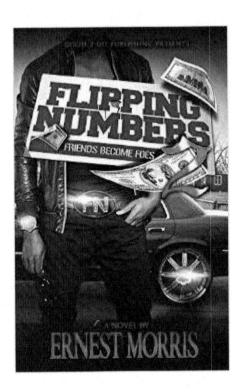

Books by Good2Go Authors on Our Bookshelf

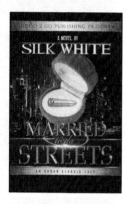

Good2Go Films Presents

To order books, please fill out the order form below:

To order films please go to *www.good2gofilms.com*

Name: _____

Address: _____

City: _____ State: _____ Zip Code: _____

Phone: _____

Email: _____

Method of Payment: Check   VISA   MASTERCARD

Credit Card#: _____

Name as it appears on card: _____

Signature: _____

Item Name	Price	Qty	Amount
48 Hours to Die – Silk White	$14.99		
Flipping Numbers – Ernest Morris	$14.99		
Flipping Numbers 2 – Ernest Morris	$14.99		
He Loves Me, He Loves You Not - Mychea	$14.99		
He Loves Me, He Loves You Not 2 - Mychea	$14.99		
He Loves Me, He Loves You Not 3 - Mychea	$14.99		
Married To Da Streets – Silk White	$14.99		
My Besties – Asia Hill	$14.99		
My Boyfriend's Wife - Mychea	$14.99		
Never Be The Same – Silk White	$14.99		
Stranded – Silk White	$14.99		
Slumped – Jason Brent	$14.99		
Tears of a Hustler - Silk White	$14.99		
Tears of a Hustler 2 - Silk White	$14.99		
Tears of a Hustler 3 - Silk White	$14.99		
Tears of a Hustler 4- Silk White	$14.99		
Tears of a Hustler 5 – Silk White	$14.99		
Tears of a Hustler 6 – Silk White	$14.99		
The Panty Ripper - Reality Way	$14.99		
The Teflon Queen – Silk White	$14.99		
The Teflon Queen 2 – Silk White	$14.99		
The Teflon Queen – 3 – Silk White	$14.99		
The Teflon Queen 4 – Silk White	$14.99		
Time Is Money - Silk White	$14.99		
Young Goonz – Reality Way	$14.99		
Subtotal:			
Tax:			
Shipping (Free) U.S. Media Mail:			
Total:			

Make Checks Payable To: Good2Go Publishing - 7311 W Glass Lane, Laveen, AZ 85339

12-16

CPSIA information can be obtained
at www.ICGtesting.com
Printed in the USA
LVOW01s2010021016
506955LV00002B/159/P